Oh, T

# Oh, Tama!

A MEJIRO NOVEL

Mieko Kanai

*translated from the Japanese by*
Tomoko Aoyama and Paul McCarthy

Stone Bridge Press • *Berkeley, California*

*Published by*
Stone Bridge Press
P. O. Box 8208, Berkeley, CA 94707
TEL 510-524-8732 • sbp@stonebridge.com • www.stonebridge.com

Except on the cover, title page, and this copyright page, Japanese names in this work are given according to Japanese convention, family name first.

First published in 2014 by Kurodahan Press, Fukuoka, Japan.

First Stone Bridge Press edition published in 2019.

Quotation from *The Waste Land* by T.S. Eliot used with permission of the author's estate and Faber & Faber Limited, London, England.

Cover illustration by Kumiko Kanai.

Cover design by Linda Ronan, incorporating Bigstock photograph © Shawn.ccf.

Printed in the United States of America.

10 9 8 7 6 5 4 3 2 1     2023 2022 2021 2020 2019

P-ISBN 978-1-61172-051-8
E-ISBN 978-1-61172-936-8

# *Contents*

# Introduction

*Tama ya* (Oh, Tama!) by Kanai Mieko is a late-twenti-eth-century masterpiece of cat literature.

Since ancient times cats have fascinated people and inspired artists and writers. There are celebrated feline protagonists and unforgettable cameo appearances of various cats in poetry, drama, fiction, art, film, manga, anime, and many other genres. There is a Wikipedia entry, a "List of cats in literature," and numerous cat-related blogs, anthologies, and studies.[1] With a few exceptions, such as Léonard Foujita and Murakami Haruki, cats in the works of Japanese writers and artists are not widely known outside Japan. However, there is indeed a long and interesting genealogy of literary cats in Japan from the celebrated example of a little Chinese cat that appears in the "Wakana" (New Herbs, or Spring Shoots) chapters (34 and 35) of *The Tale of Genji*. Murasaki Shikibu gives crucial roles to this cat, first as an accidental aid to the young Kashiwagi's obsessive longing for the Third Princess, the young wife of the middle-aged Genji, then as a consolation or substitute for that forbidden love, and finally as a symbolic premonition of the Third Princess's pregnancy with Kashiwagi's child.

Of the countless cats that appear in modern Japanese literature, arguably the three most famous are the nameless first-person narrator-protagonist of Natsume Sōseki's *Wagahai wa neko de aru* (I Am a Cat, 1905), Lily in Tanizaki Jun'ichirō's *Neko to Shōzō to futari no onna* (A Cat, a Man, and Two Women, 1936), and Nora in Uchida Hyakken's essay-like autobiographical narrative *Nora ya* (Oh, Nora!, 1957). While Sōseki's nameless "wagahai" is male, Lily is a female tortoiseshell that is the object of infatuation and undivided devotion on the part of the male human protagonist, Shōzō. Nora, on the other hand, is not a female but a male cat. He is so named because he was a stray cat, *nora neko*. However, like the heroine of Ibsen's famous play, which has had a great impact upon modern Japanese literature since the early twentieth century, this male cat Nora leaves home. Hence the distraught narrator-protagonist keeps searching for the beloved cat, desperately calling out, "Oh, Nora, Nora, where are you?"

The title of Kanai's novel is a take-off on Hyakken's title. As a cat's name, "Tama" (literally, jewel or a ball) is much more traditional and common than "Nora" or "Lily." As Kanai mentions in her "Afterword," which is also translated in this volume, almost each chapter of the original Japanese text playfully embeds "Tama" in the chapter title, while at the same time "borrowing" someone else's title. The reader will also notice that a cat called Lily makes a brief appearance in this novel; but unlike Tanizaki's coquettish female cat, this one is a male—reminding us also of Hyakken's male Nora—and suffers from diarrhea—an illness that recalls the ending of another work of Tanizaki, *Sasameyuki* (The Makioka Sisters). Kanai also makes references and allusions to other works of cat literature and their authors, such as Miyazawa Kenji and Ishii Momoko—in most cases with an ironic twist, but also with affection.

Given the breadth of her literary interests and knowledge, it is almost certainly the case that Kanai Mieko is familiar with most of the canonical cat literature, ranging from Poe and Baudelaire to Beatrix Potter's *The Tale of Tom Kitten* (1907), T. S. Eliot's book of light verse, *Old Possum's Book of Practical Cats* (1939), and perhaps the most celebrated example of cat fiction in the twentieth century, *La Chatte* (1933), by the French writer Colette. This novel describes a strange love-triangle involving the charming but immature Alain, his loving but too possessive new wife, Camille, and the cat, Saha. Alain has loved Saha since his boyhood, and, forced to choose between his wife and the beloved feline, upon whose life an attempt has been made by her human rival, decisively prefers his cat.

*Oh, Tama!* celebrates the genealogy of cat (and other) literature, and simultaneously teases out and subverts some unconscious biases and neglected issues, especially those concerning gender and sexuality, in the canonical texts. Unlike Sōseki's nameless cat, who was abandoned as a kitten, Tama has a name; and she is brought to the narrator, Natsuyuki, not as a kitten but as a heavily pregnant cat at the beginning of the novel. The themes of pregnancy and motherhood are important in the narrative. However, the mothers and the mothers-to-be in this novel, feline or human, are completely different not only from the discourse of *ryōsai kenbo* (good wife, wise mother) but also from the tropes of the eternal mother or the evil mother. Natsuyuki's nonchalant mother, for example, has almost completely forgotten about her older son, Fuyuhiko, from her first marriage. The mother of Eurasian "Alexandre" does not seem to know or care who fathered him. And Alexandre's sister Tsuneko, whose name embeds the Japanese word for a cat, *neko*, regularly uses her self-proclaimed "pregnancy" as a convenient source of income.

*Tama ya* was originally published as a series of stories, mostly in the literary magazine *Gunzō* (Group), between 1986 and 1987, and then as a hard cover in 1987 and a paperback in 1991, with a second paperback edition in 1999. For this work Kanai Mieko received the 27th Women's Literature Prize. *Tama ya* is the second book in a series of Kanai's novels that was earlier called the Mejiro Tetralogy, but with the addition of new works is now called the Mejiro Series, named after the area of Tokyo between the mega-towns of Shinjuku and Ikebukuro. The main characters (and also the author Kanai and her artist sister Kanai Kumiko, whose artwork is featured on the cover of the current volume as well as in numerous other books of Mieko) live in this area. Most of the main characters in one book appear as side characters in the others. Natsuyuki and Alexandre, for example, appear in the third work in the series, *Indian Summer* (1988), whose protagonists, Momoko, Hanako and Momoko's writer-aunt, had earlier appeared in *Oh, Tama!*

These Mejiro texts are full of humor and irony. While earlier works of Kanai, published since 1967, are noted for their surrealistic, sensuous, and poetic style and arresting, at times violent themes, the Mejiro novels focus on the human comedy in the seemingly mundane, actual world. The protagonists of the series are, however, in one way or another engaged in creative or intellectual activities, even though they are often unemployed or at loose ends. In *Oh, Tama!* Natsuyuki is an unemployed photographer and Alexandre an under-employed pornographic film star, whereas Fuyuhiko is a "fifth-grade psychiatrist" temporarily on "love sick-leave," so to speak. Intermingled with comic misadventures and layers of ambiguity created through the interactions of these characters are amusing conversations and musings about film, literature, and photography.

Kanai is a prolific and acclaimed writer not only of fiction but also of literary, film, and art criticism, with essays and commentaries on topics ranging from food, football (soccer), and fashion to philosophy, and, of course, felines. The second volume of the *Kanai Mieko Essay Collection* (Tokyo: Heibonsha, 2013) features "Cats and Other Animals." While a few of her short stories, poems, and excerpts from her longer works were translated into English beginning in the late 1970s, and attracted some attention among feminist literary scholars, this is only the third book-length English translation of her work.[2] We are certain that the reader will enjoy *Oh, Tama!* on multiple levels—as an easy, entertaining novel about a group of sometimes eccentric yet sometimes very ordinary people; as a treasure chest of rich and varied parody, allusion and intertextuality; as a text full of popular cultural icons from the 1970s and 1980s; and as a delightful example of what we may call "kiterature."

*Tomoko Aoyama*
*Paul McCarthy*

NOTES

1    Some of the studies include: Katharine M. Rogers, *The Cat and the Human Imagination: Feline Images from Bast to Garfield* (Ann Arbor: The University of Michigan Press, 1998); Kawai Hayao, *Neko damashii* (The [trickster-]cat spirit, Shinchōsha, 2000); and the feature on "Neko no bungaku hakubutsu shi" (Historia Naturalis of Cat Literature) in *Kokubungaku*, vol. 27, no. 12 (September 1982), pp.6–133. See also Ochanomizu Bungaku Kenkyūkai, *Bungaku no naka no "neko" no hanashi* (Cats in literature, Shūeisha, 1995) and *Yuriika* (Eureka), vol. 42, no.13 (November 2010) that also features "The Cat: One of the Most Familiar and Appealing yet Enigmatic and Mysterious of All Friends."

2    The first translated volume is Mieko Kanai, *The Word Book*, translated by Paul McCarthy (Champaign and London: Dalkey Archive, 2009). The second book in translation is *Indian Summer*, trans. Tomoko Aoyama and Barbara Hartley (Ithaca, NY: Cornell East Asia Series, 2012). For information on shorter translations, see Aoyama's "Introduction" in *Indian Summer*.

# Oh, Tama!

# ONE

# Oh, Tama!

Carrying a big, round-faced cat in a leather rucksack on his back, Alexandre turned up on his 250 cc motorcycle.

To keep the terrified cat from jumping out in panic, he had tied the bag's leather drawstrings so that only the cat's face protruded. Put in the oblong rucksack, the cat was forced to stand on its hind legs, a very uncomfortable posture for a four-legged creature. So as soon as the bag was put on the floor and the drawstring loosened, the black-and-white cat rushed out, keeping close to the ground, and ran into the space between the writing desk and the chair. Then, sitting with her front paws placed neatly together, she turned a steady but fearful gaze on me.

"What's with this cat?" I asked, surprised. Alexandre, mishearing, and thinking I had asked the cat's name, replied, "It's Tama—Tama-chan." Then, addressing her he said, "Isn't that right, Tama? Tama, Tama. Oh, Tama! Sweet little Tama! Now don't you worry about a thing. This nice guy here's gonna look after you, yes he is. So calm down now, calm down, okay?"

Then, talking to me again in a slightly menacing tone, "You *are* a nice guy, so you'll take her in, won't you? You'd never do something cruel like dumping a pregnant pet cat, now would you?" It sounded like a threat.

"Or are you going to say no, 'cause it wasn't you who let her get pregnant?"

He was certainly insinuating something. It occurred to me that, with this heavily pregnant cat thrust into his rucksack, Alexandre was in fact searching for the father of

Tsuneko's soon-to-be-born child. "Look, Alexandre," I said, "to be honest, I don't think I'm qualified to be a father."

"Don't worry. I know."

"Know what?"

"That you're not the father of my sister's kid," he said just like that, which relieved me but at the same time left me with mixed, ambiguous feelings.

So I said, "Why's that?" If he'd said, "It's your kid," I would have protested, emphasizing that I'd always been careful. But still it's true that we did have sex a few times—to be precise, the first time in my apartment, and the next time when I stayed overnight in her apartment, but I used—though of course I wouldn't buy those jumbo-sized packs at the Peacock Supermarket—you know, those ones that look like pretty boxes of chocolates and sit in a big basket between the sanitary napkins and the detergent shelves—those large, economy-sized boxes designed to help married couples with their family planning needs. (Yuck! They're "home products" just like cabbage, flour, miso, fish, meat, and cockroach killer.) No, but I *did* use one of the condoms I kept in the inside pocket of my jacket.

Though that morning, when we made love for the second time, still half asleep, I'm not sure if I used one. Why should I be? I know it's no use saying this now, but naturally you don't have sex for the sake of contraception. You use contraception because you need it to get sex. Besides, sexual desire (actually, all desire) is impulsive and as gooey as the inside of your mouth when you've got pyorrhea. So contraception doesn't always work, I thought, as I watched the cat crawl slowly out from under the desk, still keeping as close to the floor as possible and sniffing nervously around the strange room.

I said again, "Know what?"

"Oh, it really doesn't matter who, does it, Tama-chan?"

said Alexandre. "I'm not interested in who the father is. Are you? Does that interest you?"

"Well, . . ."

As I hesitated, he went on. "Some people even worry about who fathered *her* kittens," indicating the cat with his chin. "They'll try to guess from the colors and the patterns of their coats whether it's the orange-striped tom or the gray-and-black tabby that hangs around the neighborhood," he laughed.

"That reminds me—as you can see, me and Sis have different dads, and we've never met either of 'em. We don't care. I'm not looking for her kid's dad, though I do want to ask your advice about that later. But anyhow, for now, I just want you to look after Tama. When we found out she was gonna have kittens, we decided we couldn't keep her. You know, they say—I don't know much about these things, but they say this kind of furry animal is full of parasites—like, blah-blah-distoma, or something, isn't it? Anyway, they're no good for pregnant women. The baby might be deformed.

"That's what my aunt says, so I say to her 'Why don't you look after Tama for us then, Auntie? She's pregnant too, but those blah-blah parasites don't harm the cat itself, do they?' 'No, they don't,' she says. So then Sis says, 'Please look after Tama, Auntie,' but then she says, 'Me? Oh, no way! I was born in the year of the tiger, so I can't get along with cats. They say kittens don't do well with tiger-year people around. That'd be terrible for Tama. No, no, it'd never work. Here's a better idea, Kanemitchan. (My real name's Kanemitsu, you know.) You always wanted to have a pet cat, so why don't *you* look after her? That'd really be the best. And in return, I'll look after Tsuneko-chan's baby while she goes off to work.' And that's how I ended up with Tama.

"What's that, Tama? You're hungry? Hey, Natsuyuki,

can you open this can here? She's eating for several now, and she sure does eat a lot," said Alexandre, stroking the head of the cat, who had snuggled up to him, her long black tail up and swaying, rubbing her head against his legs and meowing loudly. "See that bag? There's a can of food and a litter box inside. Give her some food, okay? You better make friends with her right away," he said, with a serious, experienced-man-of-the-world look on his face. "Hurry up. She's hungry."

I had no choice but to hurry up and take the plastic litter box, canned food, and plastic bowls for food and water out of the old navy blue Puma sports bag that was placed just inside the door, "Now, the can opener, the can opener," I muttered as I shuffled through the kitchen drawers and shelves. I asked Alexandre if he wanted a beer.

"Why not?" he said, and, as he helped himself to a can of beer from the fridge, he added, "Oh, you've got spare ribs! Let's have some, shall we?" Shoving the ribs into the oven and pulling the tab off his can of beer, he made the usual annoying sounds with his tongue, going tchut-tchut against his palate. This alerted the cat, which was very big for a female and covered with mixed patches of black and white. She had come up meowing in quest of food, and now she pointed her ears forward and twitched her whiskers as if wondering if there wasn't a rat somewhere.

Alexandre continued his tchut-tchuting and said in a sweet voice, "Tama, you're so good at catching rats! You'll help Natsuyuki, won't you? Tchut-tchut." Then suddenly it was, like, "What's this?" and without waiting for an answer, he started to play the record that was on the turntable, turning up the volume so loud that Casals' cello resounded with a tremendous roar, which made Tama jump, so I rushed to turn it down.

"I feel like that little mouse the size of a rubber eraser that climbed inside Gorsch the Cellist's cello," I said.

Alexandre asked his usual "What's that about?" and though I tried to put him off with a bored "It's nothing," he wasn't satisfied until he got a proper answer, so I had to give a detailed explanation of *Gorsch the Cellist*. "Hmm," he said, "that sounds pretty interesting, I might read that book. Have you got a copy? If you do, can I borrow it?"

So I brought one volume of the Chikuma edition of the collected works of Miyazawa Kenji from the bookshelf and showed it to him. "What?! How come such a simple story turns into a thick book like this? Don't make me laugh. I don't have time to read this," he said, adding, "Right, Tama-chan?"

"Now, about this cat: *you* agreed to keep her, didn't you?"

"Right. Her name's Tama, by the way. That's true, but . . ."

"So why'd you bring her here?"

"That's exactly what I wanted to talk about."

"You seem to be very fond of her."

"Right, right. That's true. She's real smart, and she loves me, don't you, Tama-chan? Meow? Meow?"

"Then why?"

"Anyway, Natsuyuki, look after her. I'll come to see how she's doing once in a while."

Having gobbled up the canned food, Tama jumped lightly onto Alexandre's lap, lay down, and started to wash her face, completely settled in.

"You know about my chick, right? Well, I had to evacuate to her place—a lot of unpaid rent, skipping town—you know—but she's allergic to cats. Cat hair makes her sneeze and gives her a rash. So it's no good. 'Give away the cat and stay, or take the cat and leave: choose one or the other,' she says. Not that I'm in love with this woman, but I'm so broke that I can't find anywhere for me and Tama, with her belly full of kittens, to go. Sis can't keep the cat.

In fact, it all started with her, like I said. And my aunt says 'Oh, not with the cat, Kanemitchan.' My mom, you ask? Oh, didn't I tell you? I think it was the end of last year—she ran off with the bartender from her place, leaving all her debts unpaid. You remember, don't you? The would-be playboy, that sad old leftist, with the funny fashion sense? You had a fight with him once, remember? So I thought about asking you to let me and Tama stay with you for a while. But if the two of us are too much for you to handle, at least look after Tama for me. Think of her as a substitute for Tsuneko's baby. You know, they say it's good to be kind. Help other people. And cats. I can't trust just anyone with her, you know. There are some sickos around. When they see posters and classified ads for free kittens, they pretend they *love* cats and say things like, 'I promise I'll take good care of it. Oh, what a lovely kitten!' And then that night they slice off the kitten's ears with a utility knife in the bathroom of their apartment. It's true!"

\* \* \*

Having picked Tama up and planted a kiss on her nose, Alexandre went off. The cat nervously walked around the room, crying helplessly with an anxious look on her face, so I shut all the windows to keep her from escaping. As I worried about this and that, the phone rang. "Thanks for looking after Tama. I really appreciate it," said Tsuneko.

"Oh, that's all right," was all I could say, but I thought, *Why on earth have I got myself involved with this weird brother-sister pair?* I had a really odd feeling.

"So you *are* gonna have the baby, right?" I couldn't help asking as if to make sure.

Her response was: "Yeah, this time I'm going to. You know, lots of things happened this time, for sure. But anyway, somehow I feel it's not yours, so you don't need to worry."

Meanwhile, trying to get out the window, the cat reached out to the aluminum sash with her front paws, her claws making a horrible screeching sound, and mewed in a scared, hysterical way. On top of it all, she was going to have kittens in maybe a week or two. With the cat foisted on me like that, "You don't need to worry" didn't sound quite right to me. I had very mixed feelings.

There were some economic issues, for example. If I pawned my camera equipment, what would I do when I got a job offer? This thought worried me only for the first few days. There was no work, not even one phone call, so there was no problem with having no camera. I decided to sell some books and arranged for a nearby secondhand bookshop to come and get them.

If I sold the complete set of *The Collected Works of Miyazawa Kenji* and the box full of paperback mystery novels in the closet, I'd get a reasonable amount (only twenty or thirty thousand yen at most, though, because I'm sure the bookstore owner would say, "OK with the paperbacks 'cause they'll sell, but *this* won't sell. It'll just take up space." "Wouldn't some girl majoring in Japanese literature at Japan Women's University or Gakushūin choose Kenji for her graduation thesis and buy the set?" I'd say. But then: "No way. You're being naïve, Kobayashi-san. No one's gonna buy it 'cause students don't read books nowadays, so they don't come to my shop."

And after this exchange, *The Collected Works of Miyazawa Kenji* would be bargained down to a ridiculously low price, which, combined with the five thousand yen Alexandre handed to me with the words "This's from Tsuneko, for Tama's food" (I bet she'd given him ten thousand and he pocketed half of it), would help me get by for a while. Besides, once the secondhand bookshop took the paperbacks away, the box in the closet would be empty, which would be handy, since it could be lined with an old bath towel and turned into a place for Tama to have her kittens. So I said to Tsuneko, "How about if I put a box in the closet with a towel inside?"

"That'd be fine," she said, "since Tama's an expert in *postal matters*. She knows just what to do all on her own. But she *is* fat, isn't she, for a *postal* expert? Just like some middle-aged lady." For quite a while after this telephone conversation I couldn't figure out what she meant by *postal* expert. Did she mean Tama knew how to "post" things—like, leave her things in the right places, or what? Then, thinking hard, I realized she must have said *post-natal*, not *postal*, expert.

\*　\*　\*

Since Alexandre's morning visit had awakened me early, I had quite a bit of time before the book dealer was supposed to come. So I checked *City Road* to see what was on. The Ikebukuro Bungeiza movie house had John Huston's musical *Annie* and Robert Aldrich's *All the Marbles*, and the Takadanobaba Tōei Palace was showing Daniel Schmid's *La Paloma* and *Hécate*. Though I'd seen all four of these films before (actually, I'd seen *La Paloma* six times, *Hécate* three times, *Annie* five times, and *All the Marbles* twice), I wouldn't mind seeing them again, I thought. But the Bungeiza would charge only seven hundred yen, while the Takadanobaba Tōei Palace would cost twelve hundred, though you could get a hundred-yen discount at either place if you presented a copy of *City Road*. So, considering the current state of my wallet, *Annie* and *All the Marbles* might be the better choice, I thought.

In *Annie* (about Little Orphan Annie) the business-man played by Albert Finney, who'd adopted her on a whim, and his secretary, played by Ann Reinking, sing "Let's Go to the Movies" on their way to Radio City Music Hall to see Greta Garbo's *Camille*. I actually bought an LP of *Annie* and memorized this song. When a photographer who used to work in the same company as I did came around and saw me singing along with the record:

> "Fred and Ginger spinning madly . . .
> Songs and romance.
> Life is the dance,"

he shook his head and said, "This won't bring you work, you know. You can't just wait in the doorway doing nothing, Kobayashi. It's just like with girls. And what's with this 'bread and ginger' stuff, anyway?" Still, he did help me find a little work, and it was there that I met Alexandre.

A few years ago I applied for a job in the photography department of a publishing company that was pretty difficult to get into. I took the exam even though I thought I had no chance, it being so competitive. For some reason, I was chosen. Later I found out why: It was because the executive who conducted the job interview was such a sentimentalist. This probably wasn't due to the executive's sentimentality, but two years after I started working for the company, it went bankrupt, and they called for people prepared to take buyouts. I had no wife or children, no elderly parents, no dog or cat to support, no housing loan or other debts, so I was the first one to be tapped on the shoulder. And, since I found the work in the photography section a bore, I took their tiny buyout, and ever since I've been a freelance photographer, leading a relaxed sort of life.

Oh, yeah. Now for the reason I managed to get a job at this publishing company that was so conscientious about its business that it eventually went bankrupt. Well, this

executive named Tōdō told me some time after I started
work there, "You know, when I looked at your CV, I
thought it might just be the case . . . and I was right! You
see, a long time ago, my older brother was married to your
mother. So even though you did poorly on the exam, I let
you in—out of nostalgia. It was odd, but maybe it's karma,
I thought. My brother died about fifteen years ago, and I
wouldn't dream of criticizing your mother at this point,
but when she left, she left behind what's-his-name." (Tōdō
mentioned the name, but I've forgotten what it was.) "And
he was raised by his grandparents. He's now in the psychi-
atry section of a university hospital in Kyoto. No, not as a
patient, though it wouldn't be at all surprising if he was,
but as a doctor." etc., etc.

All this was news to me and I was taken aback, so I
talked to my mother about it. Actually, I started by asking,
"You know a Tōdō, don't you?"

"A tōdō?" she said. "A dodo is some kind of extinct
bird but . . ." She didn't seem to remember him (and she
wasn't faking it) until she heard my explanation. "Oh, yes,
of course! I completely forgot. Sorry, sorry. That's right, of
course. Before I married Kobayashi, I was married to this
man called Tōdō, wasn't I? Forgetful me!"

She laughed, which irritated me a lot. "Didn't you
have a kid from that marriage? Tche! You're unbelievable.
Forgetful doesn't half cover it! I guess it's none of my business, but he'd be my half-brother, you know."

"That's right," Mom said. "He'd be your elder brother.
What was his name, now?" I knew that was the kind of
woman she was, but I couldn't help feeling annoyed with
her, even so.

Kobayashi is my dad, but Mom left him when I was in
first grade and then got married for the third time to her
present husband, a real estate agent.

* * *

The photographer who quit the company about the same time I did was a shrewd businessman, so he changed directions and made a big splash in the spread-your-legs-and-show-it branch of the profession—the one that specializes in making you wonder if what you're seeing is pubic hair or spots on the skin or just shadows.

"I'm gonna make an adult video this time," he said. "Do you wanna work on it? It'll only take two days to make. You've seen a lot more movies than I have, so gimme a hand."

"They say making videos is easy, but the lighting and everything's completely different from stills. I've never even used an 8mm camera, so I doubt I'd be much help," I answered.

"You've seen videos, haven't you?" he went on. "Even the lighting isn't high-tech at all. An adjustable desk lamp would do, but since this is a commercial product, we'll use two or three five-hundred watt lights. Remember, we're not Godard. Don't try to be arty. We're not filming *Passion*."

"Of course not. I wouldn't dream of doing that," I assured him.

"OK, as long as you know it's not art but just a live-action sex video catering to rental shops," he insisted. So I ended up agreeing to assist, or rather, work part-time for him, not only with the actual shooting but also by editing the unbelievably bad script written with total enthusiasm by an ex-radical student activist and present freelance writer. It was a weird mixture of that idol of the leftists Takahashi Kazumi plus *Last Tango in Paris* plus Nakagami Kenji.

"As long as there's fucking scenes, the script doesn't matter," said the successful pornographer. "But this one is over-ambitious, and the relationships among the characters are totally confusing. We're gonna shoot it in two days and record at the same time, and none of our actors would be able to speak such long lines. So why don't you just leave in the porn bits and take out everything else? I'll pay you extra for doing it."

Since it was just a matter of crossing out everything except a few "lick its" and "stick it ins" with a red ballpoint pen, which only took me an hour, I earned a total of one hundred and fifty thousand yen (some of which must have come out of the pornographer's own pocket) for two days plus one hour's work. And during the filming, I got friendly with the lead actor, a Eurasian guy named Alexandre Gō.

Alexandre, talking in a rather feminine way, opined that, judging from the color of his hair (reddish brown) and eyes (light gray), his father would seem to have been a Caucasian; but he might have been a light-skinned Negro, or a Jew. He was an unspecified person whose very ethnicity was unclear.

"Can you believe even my mom has no idea who fathered her own baby!" complained this young man, who sometimes called himself an actor and at other times a fashion model or a photographer—always something different. He was what used to be called a juvenile delinquent, or in today's terms, a dropout.

"It's tough with this face and this hair to get the lowest marks in English in your junior high school. They don't take it lightly, you know," he said. Then: "Let's go to the bar my sis runs in Shinjuku!"

That's how I met Tsuneko, and one thing led to another. We didn't fall in love or anything, and after a while our relationship died down. We were just a bar owner and her customer who came in for a drink every now and then until a month ago when I was about to leave the bar and she whispered to me, "I'm five months pregnant, and I'm going to have the baby."

I said, "Wow, brave girl!" It was only when I got home that it dawned on me that it might possibly have something to do with me.

*If only Tsuneko could be as forgetful as my mom!* was the wishful thought that kept me awake that night. Then the following morning Alexandre, who, unusually for a delinquent, is an early riser, came by on his motorcycle and said in a knowing way, "There *is* a possibility that it's yours, but Sis is basically the same as Mom, in my view."

I wasn't just trying to make excuses when I told him what I suddenly and quite conveniently remembered— that I'd had mumps when I was in junior high, and I might, you know what they say, have become sterile as a result.

He said, "Yeah, that's quite possible. And you're—how shall I put it?—not the father type really." Then, wolfing down the jelly doughnuts he'd bought for me in Takadanobaba, he added, "This apartment's on the ground floor, and there's a garden right there. It's ideal for keeping a cat!" And he nodded to himself.

"So, this place is called the Red Plum Villa? And sure enough, there's a plum tree in the garden. It's well named! D'you know this haiku by Issa:

> 'On the red plum tree
> laid out to dry
> the newly washed cat'?

It was in the Japanese textbook we used in junior high. It's the only thing I still remember, for some reason. Don't you think the cat drying on the red plum tree should be black and white in this case? Ideal color coordination, eh?"

"Yeah, that'd be quite a cute scene," I found myself

saying. "The kind of Japanese cat that'd look good with a little red silk band around its neck."

"Yes—exactly! Her eyes would be glossy green like ginkgo nuts, and the pads on the bottom of her paws'd be a beautiful pink. Her muzzle would also be a moist pink, and her tail would be long and black," said Alexandre.

"Tama would be a perfect name for a cat like that," I said.

"Of course it would. Some people give pretentious names to their cats, like Mick Jagger for a tabby, or Madonna for a white cat. There's all types. Actually, I named myself Alexandre, even though my real name is Ureo. When I was born, my grandma—oh, she was a geisha in Fukagawa—probably the type that sleeps with her clients. Anyway, she was shocked because I had blue eyes, but then she said, 'Oh, well, he might grow up to be a gorgeous man like Uzaemon or Egawa Ureo.' And so they named me Ureo."

Alexander nattered on while seated on his motorcycle parked in the garden, until finally he said, "See you soon," waved good-bye, and sped off.

Being a mere mortal and not omniscient, I never guessed that this was the prelude to his bringing Tama here. And now Tama, having given up on the idea of going out, had curled up and fallen asleep, breathing peacefully. I had planned to go and see those films before the book dealer was due to come, but I changed my mind since it would be terrible if the cat, having just been brought to a strange house, got nervous while I was away and sprayed the room with her pee, with its strong clinging odor.

Even though she was a female, being this large and having both pre- and postpartum experience, she would have no compunction about lifting one hind leg like a dog and peeing away. Right now, though, she was curled up quietly on my cushion, with a blank look on her face, like that of the Virgin in Fra Angelico's famous fresco of the Annunciation.

\* \* \*

A few days later, there was a phone call from someone still hard at work in the photography section of the company that was, viewed from the outside, operating in just the same way, though on a smaller scale, even after the application of the Stock Company Reorganization and Rehabilitation Act that had been aimed at saving it from bankruptcy.

"You're quite deft in some odd specialties like producing photographic copies of plates. We have a new project that requires copies of plates—actually quite a lot of them—and I wonder if you'd do it for us."

On my way to this job, I bumped into the pornographer-photographer near the Kōjimachi intersection. "Hello! Long time no see, eh? Thanks for the work the other day."

"Hey, do you have some time? How about some coffee?" So we went into a nearby coffee shop.

"How're things lately?"

"Same as usual, but today I've got a job copying plates."

"I see. So you don't produce photographic works of your own?"

"Actually, I do sometimes, but right now my camera's in the pawnshop."

"Oh, that's no good."

"Yeah, it's a little inconvenient."

After chatting a bit this way, we started to talk about Tsuneko. He'd been a regular customer at her bar for quite a while.

"Did you know she's gonna have a baby?" he asked.

"Yeah, I think I heard something like that," I muttered and sucked noisily away at the straw in my iced coffee, which was now mostly ice cubes.

Casting a what-a-loser-you-are sort of glance at me, he asked, "Do you eat canned flaked tuna, by any chance? You smell like a cat!"

"Oh, this? You see, just before I left home, I opened a can of cat food and spilled some of it on my trousers. I wiped them with a towel, but—does it smell?" I answered.

He just nodded with an uninterested "I see" and then asked, "Whose kid could it be? I'm pretty sure it's him."

"Who?"

"Don't you know? Everyone knows. Some other names have also been mentioned, but it's got to be him."

"Is that so?" I said, which amazed him.

"You really don't know?!"

"But who is this *him*?" I said, now crunching the ice from the bottom of the glass. Crunching the ice from the bottom of a glass in a coffee shop is such a—I don't know—frustrated-youth kind of thing to do. Which reminded me—I had added a scene to that porn flick where Alexandre crunches some ice really loud and another scene where he slurps noisily away at some canned beer (which I'd plagiarized from *Stranger than Paradise*).

Anyway, the pornographer-photographer just stared at me unpleasantly through his sunglasses, nervously twitching his frizzy, pubic-hair-like mustache.

"A few names have come up as candidates for the father of Tsuneko's baby, but the unanimous favorite is a guy called Morita who owns a few buildings in Aoyama. He was there at the counter every day, you see. And the dark horse is—though apparently this one is no longer her lover—but anyway, he's an ikebana master in Ekoda. He isn't famous or anything, but they say he was the sponsor when she set up the bar. And the long shot in this race is a psychiatrist in Kyoto—he's written some books or some-thing—a dude called Tōdō, with a blank sort of look on his face. Oh, and they say he's a nephew of that idiot Tōdō at our company. You remember him. . . ."

The pornographer-photographer went on and on. Not a bad man, but a really dumb chatterbox. I truly had no idea, so I responded with *genuine* surprise: "Well, I had no idea!"

"That's the gossip of the *uninformed* customers," he added in a pleased, self-important voice.

"I see," said I. "You're so savvy, Mr. Murata."

I didn't know beans about Tsuneko's customers at the bar, but the big thick lips that she purposely emphasized with pearly purple-pink lipstick made me, and I guess everyone else—like, you know, just looking at her tongue flicking between those lips wet with saliva would remind us of the labia majora and the clitoris and would stimulate, to one degree or another, a guy's penis. And in my personal case, because she said she loved Eugene Atget's photog-raphy, I got all the more excited and told her, "Actually, when I was a student, I saved up the money I got from part-time work and bought an original print of Atget's at the Zeit-Foto Salon."

"Wow, that's fantastic! It must have been expensive," she said.

So I said, "Why don't you come over and see it?" And the reason why it didn't develop into a kind of total infatuation with daily visits to her bar might have been because sex with her wasn't as sensuous as you would have expected from those lips. Or in other words, proba-bly she didn't care much for me at all.

Besides, though I don't think I'm particularly stingy, when Tsuneko was intently scrutinizing the original Atget print, obviously wanting it badly, I sure wasn't gener-ous enough to offer her this object that I would rescue before anything else in case of fire, this single "treasury of rays" emanating from "a real body, which was there" and "ultimately touching me, who am here," showing an early twentieth-century building, now lost, and a maid in a white apron, who once lived in Paris and is shown standing inside a delicatessen. I may have misunderstood her, but she looked as if she expected me to give her the original print, which totally bewildered me.

\* \* \*

"No, not that savvy really," nodded the pornographer-photographer. Then he asked, "You're a friend of Alexandre, aren't you? Do you think he's really Tsuneko's younger brother?" This with an air of deep thought.

"I think so, though by different fathers, of course," I answered.

"I can't believe that, because her bar's been closed for two weeks now and I heard a rumor that Morita, the ikebana master in Ekoda, and the Kyoto psychiatrist were both hit for fairly large sums to cover hospital fees and immediate child-care costs. And then she moved out of her apartment without telling anyone, and I heard her bar has been leased to someone else. Alexandre said he had moved to his girlfriend's place, but no one knows where that is. So my guess is that the pair of them are in fact a couple, and they just took the money and ran. The kid in her tummy might be Alexandre's."

"Gosh, is that right?" I said, and then left for work, where in the studio I copied old film magazines and programs and developed the films, with the enlargement work left for the following day. I got off the bus in front of Mejiro Station and bought a book on cat care in the bookshop opposite the station, and then went to the basement of the building to buy superior-quality Jersey milk for the cat, some canned cat food that was on sale, and chicken rolls and some vegetables for myself. I went home to find a postcard written in terrible, almost illegible handwriting that looked like a mix of clumsy pothooks and squiggling earthworms, which said,

> Please look after Tama and her kittens. (I have a feeling that this time there'll be some gray-and-black tabbies among them.) Don't hand the kittens over to some sicko. (They get a weerd kick out of diesecting them.) Be sure to find them a good home!! ALEX

In the closet, inside a cardboard box covered with large designs of watermelons that I had been given at the greengrocer's, there were about—by my quick estimate—five newborn kittens that looked like pinkish-gray mice, being still too young to have coats with any clear colors or markings. Tama, getting upset as I looked inside the box, snarled at me, showing her fangs and fiercely wrinkling her nose, so I hurriedly shut the closet's sliding door. But I could sense her moving about trying to hide the kittens that I'd glimpsed. I'm not the type of person who talks to animals, but in this situation I couldn't help myself: "Tama, I wouldn't steal your babies."

It was an unsettling night for both Tama and me. Tama sounded as if she had fallen into postpartum depression—I read in a health column in the Sunday paper that women often suffer from this after giving birth—mewing mournfully in a hoarse, gloomy voice. She sounded as if she were pleading with me, saying, "Am I going to die? Am I? Meow? Meow?" I remembered reading that it would have a bad effect on the depressed mother if you said something like "You must pull yourself together now!" So, even though I was dealing with an animal, I tried to console her: "Tama, you're a good cat, and you're *not* going to die."

Then, while eating a chicken roll and drinking beer, I read the cat care book. The section on how to choose whom to give a kitten to had a strong warning against sickos. Meanwhile, I don't know how they got my telephone number, but men identifying themselves as Morita, Esaki, and Tōdō called one after another, each saying, "You're that Eurasian's accomplice, and you're hiding her, aren't you? Anyway, you *must* let me see her!" Each time I received one of these half-crazed phone calls, I had to read out Alexandre's postcard and let them know that it had been postmarked in Kyōbashi.

"Since she left behind the cat she loved so much, I guess she's no longer in Tokyo. She might even have gone overseas," muttered each of the despondent men, while in the closet, Tama was mournfully wailing, "Am I going to die? Am I? Meow? Meow?"

Oh, and then I remembered that the man named Tōdō must be my half-brother, so I said to her, "All three of them may be coming over here tomorrow. It's all too much, isn't it, Tama?" And I sighed.

# TWO

# The Gift

Newborn animals, their eyes still closed, look like spongy, over-ripe gourds, and can by no means be called cute. But Tama looked up at me with maternal pride as if to say, "Just watch! These kittens you think look like half-rotten gourds or miserable rats will grow cuter day by day." She would gobble down the chunks of raw tuna and chopped horse mackerel I'd bought so she'd be nourished well enough to suckle her litter of kittens. Then back she would go to the big cardboard box with the watermelon motif on the sides, and the kittens would cluster around her and guzzle her milk. And as the days passed, the creatures did somehow come to look kitten-like.

> Don't hand the kitties over to some sicko. (They get a weerd kick out of diesecting them.) Be sure to find them a good home!! ALEX

I didn't need this crappily written card from Alexandre to start searching for someone to take them. I had had that in mind ever since he'd forced Tama on me.

"Freelance photographer" sounds okay, but in fact I was jobless and unable to provide for a mother cat with a big appetite and her five offspring.

The guys who had been Tsuneko's lovers/sponsors before her sudden disappearance seemed convinced for some reason that I knew her whereabouts. I suspect Alexandre had a hand in that, but anyway, when I got phone calls from the three of them, I asked them in plaintive tones to "please take Tama's kittens off my hands. I'm not saying right now: They've only just been born and look like those unborn baby mice that the Cantonese love to eat marinated in honey. I mean after they've been weaned, of course. You're the father of Tsuneko's kid (though I don't know whether you plan to acknowledge it or not), so the least you can do is take the kittens!"

I tried to sound a little threatening midway through. I don't know if that was what did it, but Mr. Esaki, the ike-bana master from Ekoda, said, "I *love* cats, so I'll take one. Are they Persian? Siamese? Maybe Himalayan?"

"They're just garden-variety Japanese cats," I said.

"Oh, I see. Yes, they're a very good kind of cat too," he responded in a listless sort of voice. Then he started to explain his situation as if I were Tsuneko's lawyer or spokesman or something, even though we'd never even met.

By way of contrast, Morita, the owner of the build-ing in Aoyama, shouted hysterically, "It's not my duty to take on those cats!" I'd seen this dude two or three times at Tsuneko's bar—a short, stuck-up sort of guy wearing a double-breasted black doeskin suit. He liked to talk about how he was going to build a compact "intelligent build-ing" on some land in Aoyama that he was in the process of buying. "I'm trying to decide whether to have Isozaki Arata or Kurokawa Kishō design it for me," he'd brag. An absolute know-nothing, but with loads of money. A real bore. And he also seemed to think I was Tsuneko's repre-sentative or something.

"Let's be clear on this: The money I gave her was a final payment, on the condition that she wouldn't give me any trouble whatsoever about recognizing the kid at some point in the future. She was supposed to give me a written oath. Of course the kid she says she's going to have isn't mine to begin with, but I don't want any trouble later on about property rights or anything. So she agreed to that and said she'd put it in writing. But she never gave me that paper. She just took the money and disappeared!"

From his excited tone of voice I guessed that Tsuneko must have got quite a lot of money out of Morita, so I wasn't happy about the measly five thousand yen she'd given me for looking after Tama (even granting that Alexandre must have pocketed a lot before handing it over to me).

"That's got nothing to do with me. Why don't you consult a CPA or a notary public or a lawyer or a family court mediator—somebody who specializes in problems like this," I replied.

Well, this really seemed to set him off: "You ignoramus!"

So I just said, "It's really none of your business," and hung up on him.

The ikebana teacher said, "I hadn't seen her for a long time after we'd decided to call it quits, but then last year a friend of mine who didn't know anything about the two of us said he knew an amusing little bar and took me there, and it turned out to be Tsuneko's. And so we got back together again, and I said I'd help her out financially, but then she vanished without a word, I've no idea where. I gave her living expenses and money for the baby's birth, but you know, I really don't think it's my child. I don't want to go on about money matters, but I'd like to be clear on whose child it is and then decide what to do."

Well, I could tell he wasn't a bad sort of person, and he said he'd take one of the kittens when it was weaned after a month or so, so I decided to go a little further: "Don't you have some students who might want to raise a kitten? It's all I can do to care for the mother, and I don't even have time to look for someone who'll take the babies. Being a photographer, I'm away from home so much and all," I concluded.

"Isn't there some model who'd like to have a cat?" the teacher, who apparently liked nothing better than a good chat, said in a helpful manner.

"Unfortunately, I don't do fashion photography."

"Oh, so you're a socially committed sort of photographer," he said, using that out-of-date expression.

"No, not that either, really. When I was working for a company, I took all kinds of photos. In fact, I did a spread on bonsai once."

"Well, actually, you know, my school is having an exhibition at a department store soon, and perhaps we could ask you to shoot that for us?"

So I succeeded in getting rid of one kitten and getting some work for myself at the same time. I was just congratulating myself on this when another call came in from Morita, which really annoyed me, of course, and then there was a call from a man who called himself Tōdō.

This got me a little tense, and the previous two phone calls had made me uneasy too. After all, I'd forgotten to ask why they were calling *me* about all this in the first place. So that was the first thing I asked this guy Tōdō. He explained that, since Tsuneko had disappeared, he had been trying to recall the names of all the persons and businesses that had come up in his earlier conversations with her, making a list of them, looking up their phone numbers, and then calling each and every one of them.

In this process, he remembered Tsuneko's younger brother Alexandre and his girlfriend, whom he'd been introduced to at Tsuneko's bar at one point. He didn't know Alexandre's surname, so there was no way of finding his telephone number. His girlfriend, though, had said she was a fashion model. "But a girl can't make a living doing that, so I'm, like, working part-time at this mini-club on the Ginza. Here's the name of the club—drop by some time!" she said, giving him a lavender business card with little wave-like patterns incised along the edges. He couldn't quite recall which suit he was wearing at the time, but he had the habit of putting business cards into the breast pockets of his suits and leaving them there until it was time for the suits in question to be sent to the dry cleaners. ("I'm not a methodical person. . . .") He thought the card must be in one of those suit pockets, searched for it, and sure enough! There it was in the breast pocket of a gray between-seasons suit coat. So he knew he must have met them in June of last year. On the lavender business card with its wave-like incised edges was the name of the bar, La Mauve, together with a drawing of a seagull.

Then he gave this interminable explanation of how he happened to call me: "I knew they wouldn't be answering the phone until evening, so it made more sense just to go there directly. I took the Shinkansen super express from Kyoto and found the bar near Ginza. 'Is there a young lady named Aoi here?' I asked, and a woman who seemed to be the 'mama' of the bar—just when did we start to call women bar owners 'mama' I wonder—found time to talk with me since the place was not yet at all crowded.

"'Aoi quit some time ago. She was much brighter than she looked. She knew that La Mauve was French and meant "hollyhock" as well as "seagull," so she said she'd take the name "Aoi" for hollyhock to use here. Imagine that!' And on she chattered: 'But that boyfriend of hers was no good. Half-caste, scrounging around for money . . . By the way, Doctor'—I'd given her my card so she called me that—'she seemed a little strange. Did she run away from your hospital or something?'

"It took some time to answer all the mama's questions, but at last she gave me a telephone number. 'I imagine she might still be at this number,' she said. So I called, and she was there. But when I asked about Alexandre, she yelled, 'I don't know anything about that son of a bitch. How should I know where he lives?' Then she slammed down the phone. Well, I called again, and after a lot of fussing she gave me the phone number of 'the director of a sex video that s.o.b. was in. The director asked me to be in it too and gave me his card, just in case. I guess *he* might know.' So I called him and he told me about you, who're such a good friend of Alexandre's."

Later it occurred to me that this dogged manner of Tōdō's had nothing in common with Mother's character, so it must have been due to nurture rather than nature in his case.

I told him that Alexandre had left the cat and gone who knows where. But, just as I suspected, he kept on asking if I knew where he was likely to have gone. So I told him, "If Alexandre contacts me, I'll tell him about you."

"Please don't just tell him about me. Try to arrange a meeting between us," he shot back. "Perhaps I shouldn't say this, but Alexandre seems to be the kind of guy who wouldn't bother to get in touch with me even if you gave him my message."

Well, there was no denying that, but I told him that I had no way of knowing when Alexandre might contact me. "And besides, you live in Kyoto, don't you?"

"Yes, that's true, but I plan to be in Tokyo for a while," he said, giving me the telephone number of the hotel he was staying at. "At any rate, I absolutely have to see Tsuneko," he concluded.

I hung up the phone without saying, as I wanted to, "Everybody's looking for her!"

Then I remembered that this guy must be my half-brother. Tomorrow they might all show up in my room. "Oh, Tama, what a mess!" I sighed, and out she came from her cardboard box and proceeded to not so much lap up as gulp down the superior-quality Jersey milk (485 yen a carton!) I had bought for her. "Miul," she said in a some-what hoarse voice, returning to her kittens with an air of satisfaction.

Anyway, I'd have to go to the company tomorrow and print photos from the film I had copied. Enlarging copies from old magazines and commercial photos of film stars required delicate adjustments for each and every one, or the moiré patterns would make it look terrible. It was more trouble than you might think, and it had to be done in the morning. That meant getting up early, and I hadn't had to do that since losing my job, so I'd have to get to sleep nice and early.

It made me tense to think I'd have to be asleep by midnight, so I made sure the closet doors were open twenty centimeters or so to permit Tama free exit and entry, then got into bed and started to read with a whiskey and soda for a nightcap. But then there was a phone call from Mother saying that her third husband, the real estate agent, had collapsed in the toilet that evening and been taken by ambulance to the hospital. "It's a heart attack. The doctor says he isn't in any immediate danger, but I'm pretty down. Could you come over?

"Yeah, that's right. I'm just back from the Ebara Hospital. He'll be in the hospital for some time, I suppose. Anyway, I'm feeling down, so could you come over and stay here for a while? I've got to be at the hospital tomorrow, and it'd make me feel better just to know you were here at home."

Her voice sounded all trembly and tearful, so I tried to calm her down: "I'll be there tomorrow afternoon, then. Since the doctor's saying nothing's gonna happen today or tomorrow, I don't think you have to worry, Ma." Then I added, "What about his life insurance?"

"There're four policies, I think—one of them with you as beneficiary. I told him to do it that way. One of them's in my name, and the other two are for his kids by his ex-wife. But Atsushi and Kiyoto are going to get the company, so maybe I should get him to change the insurance policies. Put 'em in your name. It should be about fifty million altogether," she said.

"And in return I'm supposed to look after you?"

"Well, with that kind of money you should be able to set up that rental studio you were talking about, and you wouldn't have to work hard at all."

"It's not that simple," I answered and then went on. "By the way, I just had a phone call from my older brother—the one you left behind at Mr. Tōdō's in Kyoto."

"Oh, my God! One shock after another today! And what did he want, this . . ." She mumbled a bit.

I could tell she'd forgotten the name of her own child, so I helped her out: "Fuyuhiko, isn't it?"

"Yes, that's it! Fuyuhiko—winter child. Your older brother's named Fuyuhiko. That's why I called you Natsu-yuki—summer boy." She laughed merrily.

"So what about Fuyuhiko? What did he say about me?" Her voice had gone teary again.

"He said he'll never forgive you for what you did."

"No, I suppose not!" she said in a dramatic voice. "Anyway, be sure and come over tomorrow night. I'll explain everything." Then, as usual, having said what she had to say, she hung up abruptly. I got out of bed and poured myself another glass of whiskey. And, while listening to Tama keeping up her sad-sounding, hoarse mewing, as if she was suffering from postpartum depression—though God knows she was eating like a horse!—I wondered to myself why all these troublesome things had to happen to me all at once.

"Heeyy, am I about to *die*, do you think?" Tama seemed to be asking. I didn't have the energy even to say, "Oh no, Tama, you're a good cat. You're not gonna die."

Instead I shouted, "I'm gonna get rid of that damn box and you and your kittens right along with it!" Then Tama became strangely quiet, but I still couldn't sleep. Finally, when I was just drifting off, the phone woke me up again. The alarm clock by my pillow said 2:15 a.m. I figured the real estate agent had died, so I answered the phone.

"Did Tama give birth okay?" It was Alexandre's voice, and it sounded very relaxed and happy.

"Yeah, she did," I answered crossly. "Five kittens."

"Really? That's great! But you sound as if you've got a cold or something, Natsuyuki. Where's that old energy? Or are you drunk? You're the type that gets moody when they drink. Anyway, I plan to come over sometime soon to see Tama and the kittens. Take good care of them now, won't you?" he concluded.

"What the hell's going on? I've been getting phone calls from all over asking where Tsuneko is, and it's a damn nuisance, let me tell you!" I shouted into the phone.

But Alexandre seemed totally unfazed: "How should I know where she is? If what you say is true, I'd like to find her myself and get some money out of her."

He didn't seem to be lying, so I contented myself with saying that I'd begun to find homes for the kittens and that if he didn't come and get Tama soon, I'd have her sterilized before she went into heat again.

"Eh? What was that you just said?"

"What I'm saying is that, whether Tama is your cat or Tsuneko's, as long as I have to take care of her, I've decided to have her spayed."

"You can't do that! How could you think of doing such a cruel, selfish thing? To an innocent animal!"

"If you're going to talk like that, do it when you're looking after her yourself!" I retorted.

"But I explained why I can't do that already! I only asked you because there was no other way, you son of a bitch!" Alexandre went on the attack in this childish or, shall I say, not-so-bright way.

"Well then, come over right now and take the whole kit and caboodle, including the kittens!"

Alexandre, ignoring this reply of mine, continued, "Hey, Natsuyuki, you're a bright guy, so I bet you read the op-ed columns in the *Asahi* daily, right?" I was at a loss, since he'd changed the subject so suddenly. "Well, I don't know who the writer was, but probably somebody big, and he wrote it right in there: Urban pet owners who have their pets neutered are being really egotistical. And he's right, you know. They're animals, after all, and their instinct for self-preservation makes them have kids. So is it okay to rob them of that, just 'cause it's more convenient for humans? That's what this big writer said. And isn't he right? Like, we gotta have a sense of responsibility for the new life that's coming along. Like, if you kill some kittens with your own hands, you gotta live with that pain for the rest of your life, man!"

Alexandre's sudden conversion to humanitarianism, or reverence for life, or whatever it was, made me mad.

"Listen, you. Get your ass over here and pick up these damn cats! I'm gonna leave them and their box outside my window for you!" I shouted and slammed down the phone.

God, what a mess! I must have wasted around four hours on the phone that day. "Pick up these damn cats!" I'd yelled, but Alexandre, being the lowlife he was, would never come to pick up Tama and the kittens no matter how close he might have been to where I lived. And I didn't even know where he was, for starters. So of course I didn't actually put out the box Tama and her kittens were sleeping in.

What I needed was some shut-eye. I looked at the clock near my bed and saw it was 2:45 a.m. I figured I'd spend at least another hour tossing and turning in bed before I got to sleep, and I knew I had to be at this company's darkroom in Kōjimachi by 9:00 to start work on the enlargements, which meant I'd have to leave here by 8:15. What with washing my face, eating breakfast, and opening the can of food for the cat, I'd need to get up by 7:30 at the latest. So I'd only get three and a half, or four at the outside, hours of sleep. Good God! For a guy with low blood pressure like me, that's absolutely not enough shut-eye. I kept on fretting over the situation until I heard the sound of a newspaper being stuffed into the mail slot in my door. The pale bluish light of dawn shone through the gaps in the curtains, and I heard the sound of my landlord's elderly wife, who lived in the next building over, sliding open their shutters.

"We quit taking the paper last month! Why do you keep delivering it every morning? We've made it clear we're not interested anymore, so there's no point in you coming to collect the fee. We won't pay! You just keep on delivering it for some reason." She scolded on in a shrill voice that carried a lot further than you'd expect coming from a little old lady. The paperboy must have been one bewildered-looking kid, since he wasn't making deliveries to the landlord's house anymore.

"I'm not delivering it. . . ."

"Why, it's in our box every morning! And look, here. I've even put up a notice for you to stop."

"Yeah, that's why I'm not delivering it anymore."

On it went, and I wasn't about to butt in. The fact was, though, that my slightly senile landlord was silently taking the newspaper out of my mail slot every morning. So I asked the paperboy not to leave it half sticking out of the slot since "it sometimes gets stolen" but to push it all the way in. "Yes, sir, I will!" said the rather stylish lad, with his red Converse basketball shoes, carefully unmatched green and blue left and right socks, and black ixi:z track suit. But he didn't. So every morning the old guy would come and take my paper and go read it in his living room.

"What? That paper's been delivered again? We can't have that!" I imagined the old lady saying. I never read the paper anyway, though, and if I did speak to her about it, she'd be like, "Why, I never realized! I'm so very sorry. My husband's mind is going, I'm ashamed to say," using the out-of-date refined speech of the "high city." Then she'd wrap up some Korean jelly candies and candied pomelo peel that someone had sent from Kumamoto in Kyushu, her husband's hometown, and bring it over. "Please try this. I don't know if it'll appeal to a young person like you—it's such a provincial sort of sweet, I know." With this as an intro, I was sure I'd be treated to "This Woman's Life: The Unsolicited Confessions of a Landlady," so I didn't really want to raise the matter at all.

But there was another reason why I'd never said anything about her husband walking off with my daily newspaper: When I ran into him in the garden, he seemed to mistake me for his grandson. "Oh, you here again, son? Now don't say anything to Granny about this—not a word now." And he'd pull a thousand-yen note from the pocket of the thick woolen trousers he wore even in summer. "You just take this," he'd say, pressing the bill into my hand.

At first I was surprised and muttered, "Oh, no, I couldn't. I don't need it, really."

"Never mind, never mind. Just buy yourself some nice eel or sweet bean soup or something," he'd answer and force me to take the money. So I'd accept it, and then later explain to his wife that he seemed to take me for his grandson and return the money to her. But, considering that on a few occasions I had kept the thousand-yen bills the old guy insisted on giving me, it seemed better to let the matter of the newspaper rest. But when the old lady *did* find out about it, there'd be a lot of explaining to do, I felt. What a situation! Anyway, I figured I could still get maybe two hours of shut-eye so I pulled the blanket up over my head. After what felt like maybe five minutes, the alarm woke me up.

It hadn't been raining earlier, but now I could hear the soft, wet sound of rain falling outside the window. A famished Tama was meowing in a very demanding way, rubbing her head and face against the kitchen door and the table legs and flicking her erect tail slightly from side to side. I recalled having seen just the same kind of behavior a long time ago.

The name wasn't Tama. Lily was an orange male tabby who, as long as he was with me, produced diarrhea of the same color as his fur, with which he soiled the cushions, bedding, and cardboard boxes containing my books and film. Why was this diarrhea-afflicted cat staying with me? you ask. His owner brought him to me.

"Lily's problem is nerves," she said. "He takes after me. That's why he's so high-strung."

"I bet he's just scarfing down half-rotten garbage from somewhere."

She was outraged at this. "You really know how to get on a person's nerves, don't you?"

"You think so?"

"Yes, I do!"

It looked like she had no intention whatsoever of cleaning up after Lily, so I had to get some tissues out and do the job, but the smell still lingered in the room. . . .

We had met at the opening party for a photographer friend's private exhibition; somebody introduced me to this "woman poet." Her hairstyle was super-feminine, with loads of curls. Her dress revealed a lot of her back, so her flat, freckled shoulder blades were plain to see. Yet the front of the dress was all frilly and girlish. Her skirt was very tight and hip-hugging, slit about twenty centimeters above the hollows behind her knees. The result was that when she bent over even a little, you could see the stitching on the thigh area of the panties she was wearing under her pink polyester knit dress. And now here she was, sleeping naked on the bed in my room! A close inspection revealed pale brown freckles not only on her shoulder blades but on her flat breasts, on her nose and under her eyes in spots where the makeup had come off. With the very feminine dress off, she looked quite . . . rugged, should I say? or downright masculine.

After she woke up she wrapped a sheet around herself, went to the toilet, took a shower, and then had a cup of the black tea I'd made.

"What's that?" she asked, pointing at a tree with pale violet flowers that was blooming in the garden, there in the rain.

"Lilacs—

> April is the cruelest month,
> breeding Lilacs out of the dead land, mixing
> Memory and desire, stirring
> Dull roots with spring rain.

"*That* lilacs," I answered gloomily.

"What's that? A poem by you? Do you write poetry too? The one you just quoted? It's really good!" Then, cocking her head a bit to one side as if deep in thought, she made this critical comment: "A little clichéd in spots, though . . . "

"Yeah, well, it's a really long poem, you know."

"Let me read it!"

"Sure, but I've put it away somewhere—don't know where right now. There was another line I remember: You, hypocrite reader—my double, my brother!"

"It's a pretty tragic-sounding poem."

"Yeah, I guess so."

She laughed happily and said, "Well, I've got to be going! Will you come with me as far as the taxi stand?" So I went with her to Mejiro Avenue, then returned to my room and started to reread Eliot's *The Waste Land* in Yoshida Kenichi's translation, which I'd bought at a used bookstore some time before. As I read, I fantasized about creating a collection of photographs taken in London in black and white, in homage to *The Waste Land*, though looking back on it now, I realize how anachronistic, vulgar, and just plain stupid that would have been. Eliot dedicated *The Waste Land* to "Ezra Pound, a better poet than I am." I wanted to dedicate my photo collection to "Robert Bresson, who taught us through images that stoicism is itself the most radical and unfortunate form of desire." But if I was going to dedicate it to Bresson, I thought perhaps I should take the photos for *The Waste Land* in color, in homage to *Four Nights of a Dreamer*, with its famous color emulsion that glistens in flesh tones, smiling triumphantly. As I fantasized away, I got excited, and my thing, which I really do believe I hadn't used the night before, suddenly got hard.

That night, the woman poet came back with a light blue suitcase and her cat named Lily. For a week or maybe ten days, she and her cat stayed with me. Apparently, she read the copy of *The Waste Land* that was on my desk. "Liar! That poem you said you wrote? You plagiarized it from Eliot, didn't you?"

"I thought you'd know it was from Eliot. You're a poet, aren't you?"

Well, that made her mad, and she turned aside with a "Hmph!" Just then, this dark chubby guy, who seemed to be her husband or her lover or, anyway, the guy she was living with, appeared. How the hell did he find the place?

"What's this about?" he said in a low, tense voice and with a brooding stare. Then he settled himself on the narrow veranda in total silence. The woman didn't say anything either, just sat there sideways in a relaxed sort of way, her face averted. I didn't have anything in particular to say either, so I just sat silently gazing at the two of them. After an hour or so had passed, a guy who had been my classmate in photography school and who was living in Minami Nagasaki came along—oh yeah, he was the one who'd introduced me to the woman poet to begin with— and with his sharp intuitive skills figured out something was wrong.

"It was weird, man, weird! This woman and her husband and Natsuyuki spent one whole evening in a silent three-sided deadlock," he later told everyone, and as a result I was privately referred to as "three-sided-deadlock Natsuyuki" for quite a while. Finally, at some point in the second hour, the woman and her husband left, still without saying a word. They left Lily behind, and I haven't heard from them since.

The woman poet had referred to the color of Lily's coat as "carrot" or "marmalade" or "whiskey." But, if you ask me, it was actually "diarrhea color." That's what I'd call it.

Lily never seemed to get used to me. When I came near, he'd arch his back and run away. Yet for some reason he settled right into my apartment, so what could I do?

I remembered reading a long time before in *Tom of the Hill* about a country vet who advised mixing powdered charcoal into the food of a cat with chronic diarrhea. So I asked for a piece of charcoal from my landlord's wife. (She taught tea ceremony).

"Will just one do? What are you going to use it for?"

"Oh, I thought I'd put it in the teakettle and try to get rid of the smell of chlorine from the water that way."

"My, aren't you a clever young man to know about that!"

So I pulverized the charcoal and sprinkled a lot on Lily's food. His nose and mouth looked a little dirty, but the diarrhea stopped. Then the mating season came and off he went, never to return.

\* \* \*

The enlargements of the prints I was doing at my part-time job were relatively simple to do. I was also doing enlargements from some moldy old rolls of film that a film critic had taken in Paris way back. I was startled to see a snapshot of Anna Karina, smiling in front of a mirror as she put her hair up, emerge onto the photosensitive paper under the light of the enlarger. Great numbers of snaps of Anna Karina in various poses were preserved on that moldy Kodak film. Entranced, I went on enlarging them. In the tray filled with acidic-smelling fixer, through that slightly shifting membrane, slowly, gradually, Anna Karina revealed her smile, misty, cloud-like. I was in ecstasy!

I wasn't the one who'd taken the photos, yet I felt as if I were the possessor of this Venus emerging from the fixer. I decided that I would take home with me the 5 x 7 photos of Anna Karina that I had so painstakingly printed for myself without asking the photographer's permission. It was then that I suddenly had the somewhat gloomy sense that I may have been cut out to be a top-notch darkroom technician rather than a photographer.

But I had no time to wallow in that gloomy feeling, for a great stroke of luck came my way. Having just finished my work in the darkroom, I happened to run into a former colleague, a real loser of an editor. In fact, I can't for the life of me figure out why he wasn't fired before anyone else in the company. Anyway, he treated me to lunch, so,

by way of repayment, I showed him the photos of Anna
Karina. "If you really want one, I could give one to you,"
said I, impressing on him that I was doing him a favor.

"Don't know her. Must be some movie star from the
old days," he just said in an adenoidal voice. So I made
sure to order, at his expense, a large draft beer in addition
to the chicken set lunch. I listened patiently to his whin-
ing about how tough it was for companies that had fallen
under the Stock Company Reorganization and Rehabilitation Act, and then said goodbye.

I telephoned Mother. "Oh, Natsuyuki, Dad died this
morning. Come on over right away. The body's just come
from the hospital, and the wake will be tonight."

\* \* \*

To tell you the truth, the first thing I thought of was
the insurance money. As a matter of fact, I'd been wanting to use it to go to New York for quite some time. I
was only nineteen or twenty when I'd been thinking about
taking the *Waste Land* photos in London. Later I got
really interested in the photos of Coney Island taken by
the not-too-well-known photographer Amanda Anderson when she was a girl. And I wanted to take pictures
of Coney Island myself, though of course it must have
looked entirely different from the way it looked back in
her day. And I wanted to meet this lady named Swanson,
who was Anderson's biographer and edited a book called
*Amanda Anderson: Her Photographs and Life*, which was
put out by Philomela Press, a little-known publisher in
Boston. And I wanted to have Ms. Swanson show me a
particular photo—one not in the book—that Amanda had
referred to in a note. It was a strange combination of "a
bear, an Indian, a little girl, and a donkey," a pornographic
photo that represented "a highly improper utopia . . . one

fragment of a somewhat grotesque nightmare," to borrow Ms. Swanson's words. Above all, I wanted to get my hands on some of Amanda's original prints. Then I wanted to make enlargements of them myself.

Now, thanks to the insurance money, all this might be possible, I thought, and that was surely a stroke of luck! So I went back to the Red Plum Villa, planning on going from there to the wake, only to discover from beyond the garden hedge that a light was on and the curtains open in the room whose window I had left open a bit so Tama could come and go, but whose curtain I was sure I'd drawn before leaving. Not only that, but I could see Alexandre and someone who was a complete stranger to me sitting across from one another at my table, with cups of tea and pieces of cake in front of them. And as for Tama, she too was on the table, drinking a saucer of milk.

As I looked in disgust from beyond the hedge at this scene in my room, Alexandre noticed I was there. "Heeyy, welcome home! What are you doing out there? Come on in! We've been waiting for you all this time. Oh, and there was a telephone call from your mom. She's a little odd, isn't she? Can't she tell the difference between her son's voice and somebody else's? 'Hello,' I say, and she's like, 'Dad's dead!' So I say, 'I'm not Natsuyuki.' And she says, 'Don't joke with me at a time like this!' And she's, like, shouting at me all of a sudden. Do you usually play jokes on your mother on the phone or something?" he asked in a loud voice over the windowsill.

I went into my room and said, "What's all this about? Did you come for the cat?" Alexandre didn't respond to that.

"This is Mr. Tōdō. Say, explain to him that I don't know where Tsuneko is right now, will you?" Alexandre said, jutting his unshaven jaw in Tōdō's direction.

I sighed.

"Want some tea?" suggested Alexandre.

"Yeah."

Mr. Tōdō, rising from his seat and taking a business card out of his jacket's breast pocket, offered it to me saying, "Excuse me for calling so suddenly the other day." Then, with a haggard look on his face, he continued, "I'm taking a week off from the hospital without permission, so I may have been fired already, but . . ."

"I see," I said, without meaning anything at all, and gave a nod.

"Where the hell could she have got to, that woman!" interjected Alexandre. "Anyway, you're going to the wake, aren't you, Natsuyuki?"

"I'm planning to. What are you and this gentleman going to do?"

"Hmm. Well, I'll wait here for you to get back. I don't have any plans—lots of time on my hands lately. But I suppose *he*'ll be going home."

Suddenly I felt very tired. I gazed at my half-brother, who seemed to be totally unaware that that's what he was. Dazed as I was, I became aware that Alexandre had decided to settle down there in my room.

"It'll be hard on you if you're going to come back here for the night. I'll have supper ready for you," Alexandre offered.

I don't know why, but I found myself saying, "No, never mind. There'll be sushi or something at the wake. I'll bring some home with me."

Alexandre and Mr. Tōdō both nodded at the same time, as if to say, "Oh, that's a good idea!"

# THREE

# Amanda Anderson's Photographs

We—by which I mean Tama, who happily stayed on in my apartment, her kittens, Alexandre, and my older half-brother Tōdō Fuyuhiko—spent the long, dull, rainy days of April together, doing nothing in particular.

"So, what are you two planning on doing?" I asked.

To which Alexandre responded: "I'm sorry, but please put me up for a while, 'cause I have nowhere else to go. Besides, I can be useful. I can look after Tama and answer your phone while you're out working. Plus, I can be your assistant, carry your camera stuff for you." As he spoke, he cast a sidelong glance at Fuyuhiko as if to say, "*I* can be useful, but what can this 'fool in love' do for you, eh?" Then, with a wink, he whispered to me, "Let's get rid of him."

On the second morning after they came to stay, Alexandre addressed "the lover" while munching on a piece of toast slathered with butter and honey. "Listen, hanging around with me isn't gonna get you any word from Tsuneko, you know. She's not that kind of woman. Ma isn't, and neither is she. Besides, sorry to point this out, but the father of her baby-to-be could be you, or it could be somebody else entirely. So, it's like, even Sis has no idea whose kid it'll be. Hey, hey, cool it, will ya? I'm right, aren't I, Natsuyuki? You were scared it might be *yours*, now weren't you?"

"That's beside the point," I said. "Hey, don't wave your toast around like that while you're talking. You'll drip honey all over the floor!" Then, giving some milk and cooked chicken liver to Tama, who had just emerged from the cardboard box in the closet that served as her maternity-ward-cum-nursery and who was now meowing and rubbing her head against my shins, I said to Alexandre, for the fifteenth or maybe fiftieth time, "If you know where Tsuneko is, why don't you just tell him?"

\* \* \*

"Look, I can't tell him what I don't know! If I knew, of course I'd tell him." Alexandre repeated the same old answer he'd already given fifteen or maybe fifty times, but this time in a strange Kansai accent, which I found a little irritating and frustrating. But just as when he'd forced the care of the pregnant Tama on me, I couldn't find any real reason to protest. And I couldn't manage to throw my two unwelcome guests out, either. Newborn kittens, their eyes still closed, look like spongy, over-ripe gourds and can by no means be called cute. But Tama looked up at me with maternal pride as if to say, "Just watch! These kittens you think look like half-rotten gourds or miserable rats will grow cuter day by day." Perhaps due to postpartum exhaustion, her voice was a little hoarse: "Bimeowm."

The newborn kittens that looked like rotten gourds or small leeches might well become cuter as time went by. Meanwhile the man who had somehow come to stay seemed like a rotten gourd or a leech that had taken the form of an adult male.

That may sound like an overstatement, but isn't it true that a man in love is as disgusting a thing as that? This lump of pink desire, wasting away yet still upright—this tired, dirty fellow, unshaven and unwashed for three or four days—I looked at him with a mixture of sadness, pity, and disgust and wondered how on earth such a man could ever have managed to work as a psychiatrist, even the most incompetent one.

To complicate things more, Fuyuhiko still didn't realize that we were half-brothers, and under the circumstances I wasn't sure whether I should tell him or not. Needless to say, I don't like thinking about troublesome or complicated matters, and when I do think about them, it makes me sleepy. Anyhow, in the end it turned out that there was no need to worry. As they say, easier in the doing than worrying about it beforehand. Leaving a blank-faced Fuyuhiko sitting alone in the room, Alexandre and I went out to do some shopping at the supermarket and then dropped in at the public bath. Meanwhile, my mother rang, assumed as usual that the person picking up the phone must be me, and began talking.

"It was such a shock! You know, just when Father [that's how my mother referred to her third husband, who *wasn't* my father] died, you told me you'd met Fuyuhiko. It was one shock after another! I wonder how he is. It's been more than thirty years since I left Tōdō, you know. You told me Fuyuhiko said that he'd never forgive me, but I can't believe that. That couldn't be true, could it? I'm his mother, after all, so he'll understand. I'm sure he will." She went on and on, without waiting for any response from the other end, and as he listened to her chatter, Fuyuhiko must have caught on to the dramatic fact.

"Could such a coincidence be possible?!" said Fuyuhiko, looking at me in an agitated way when we returned after having had a bath and then some beer at a noodle shop. Alexandre, who always liked to meddle in other people's affairs and insisted on knowing everything, interrupted his story of a man with two penises, whom he claimed to have seen in a public bath in Jiyūgaoka when he was a child. (On our way home he had persisted, though I told him he must have been mistaken.)

"What's the matter? Did Tsuneko call or something?" he asked. Fuyuhiko ignored that question and started explaining about Mother's telephone call. Hearing his story, Alexandre just shook his head and said, "My, oh my! Well, whaddaya know?"

\* \* \*

"My, oh my!" he continued. "That's unbelievable. But women are like that, aren't they? I don't know what kind of horrible things my dad might have done in Vietnam, and Ma probably doesn't even know who my real dad was anyway. Right, Tama? Just like you. Or do *you* know?"

"I wonder . . . ," said Fuyuhiko. "Animals—well, I'm not too sure about cats, but I wonder if they have sex with just any old cat during the mating season. Isn't it just human beings that do things like that?"

"Yeah, well, just once is enough to get a female pregnant, so maybe she wouldn't let any male near her after that," said Alexandre, looking impressed. He stroked Tama's head. "Well, well, you've got your own kind of fidelity, don't you now?" Tama responded with a hoarse "bnew" and hurried back to her cardboard-box nursery.

"So this is a meeting of long-lost brothers," Alexandre whispered to me, snickering as he put the contents of the plastic shopping bags from the supermarket into the refrigerator. "But in this case, you two are 'cock brothers' as well, since you've both screwed the same woman. Not that that's a big deal."

\* \* \*

Fuyuhikos's new-found understanding of the situation

did not really change anything. Apparently believing that if he stuck close by Alexandre, there would be some sort of word from Tsuneko, Alexandre's sister, he showed no signs of leaving my apartment; he seemed, rather, to settle in. Alexandre would explain to him, "All right, my sister might contact me sometime, but no one knows when that sometime might be. On the basis of my twenty-odd years of relating to her as family, I have no idea when that will be. Since she was in junior high, she's left home and then come back without warning any number of times, and I never wasted time wondering when she might be back.

"And you know, to tell you the truth, it's all a lie about her having a baby. She's been doing this all over Japan for years now. It's kind of like a swindle—no, it actually *is* a swindle: telling some guy she's pregnant so she can get money off him and then run. I'm telling you this because you're Natsuyuki's brother. You'd better give up and forget about Tsuneko. Otherwise you'll ruin yourself. Go on back to Kyoto and make a fresh start."

He'd try to spoon-feed Fuyuhiko with advice like this, but his plan for himself was to stay with me "for the time being." Reclining at his ease in the room facing the garden, he grumbled about having no money and being unable to go out on the town. Plucking some hairs from his nostrils with a thumb and forefinger, he gazed at the cherry tree, which looked a bit dreary due to the long rains and cloudy weather. "Let's have a cherry-blossom-viewing party in the garden when the weather improves," he suggested. "There's that poem:

'The colors of the flowers have faded
as in idle thoughts
my life passes sadly by
while I watch the long rains fall,'"

quoting Ono no Komachi's poem inaccurately.

And Fuyuhiko, for his part, would say, "You know, that sounds all right. Not doing anything in particular, just looking at the cherry blossoms, I might be able to get over this pain, in time. They say, 'Oblivion means forgetting things completely,' and 'Time heals all wounds.' So if I go back to the university as if nothing had happened and churn out about ten research papers and keep myself occupied, someday I might meet Tsuneko again by chance somewhere. I'm sure I will! And she'll just smile at me like always without a word of explanation—as if we'd parted only yesterday and were meeting again today. She'd say with a bright smile, 'I've told you a hundred times: your necktie is always off-center.'" There were sighs mixed in with all this, and he ended by promising to adopt a black-and-white kitten with a long tail, the very image of Tama, on the basis of it being "a child of the cat that Tsuneko had loved."

Meanwhile, the cameraman who used to work at the same company as I did had introduced me—this former colleague, now a successful adult video producer, said that I "just might be better suited to writing than to taking photographs." Anyway, he had introduced me to someone called Watabe, who knew all sorts of people from his experience working in various industries. He ran a somewhat dubious photography magazine sponsored by a guy who seemed to have made a pile from wheeling and dealing in real estate and finance companies. I'd agreed to write something on Amanda Anderson for their special issue on "Unknown Artists."

"Sorry we can't pay much," Watabe said. It was 1,000 yen a page, and according to the adult video maker, it was quite conscientious of Watabe to let me know the rate beforehand. "It might be a low rate, but, unlike so many in this business, at least Watabe won't stiff you when the work is actually finished," he added.

So, opening my copy of *Amanda Anderson: Photographs and Life* (Boston: Philomela Press) by Gloria Swanson, which I had found at a secondhand bookshop in Hong Kong several years earlier, I struggled to write something on the manuscript paper that I'd placed on the table in my small kitchen (the room facing on the garden being under occupation by my two "guests"). But Alexandre came and complained: "There's no space here, Natsuyuki, for that sort of work. If I stand at the gas ring to put a kettle on or whatever, my ass'll be brushing against your back. It's nearly time for me to cook supper, so why don't you move over?" Then, picking up *Amanda Anderson: Photographs and Life* from the tabletop and browsing through it, he said, "Looks kind of interesting. Who was this photographer?"

"You can read my article when it's published. And if you're that interested, would you be so kind as to shut up and let me write?" I answered.

"Oh well, it's your apartment after all. You don't need to pretend to be so humble. But why can't you tell me now? You know I can't read a word of English. Besides, who knows? As you explain it to me, you may get some ideas for your piece." To me, his tone was—how shall I put it?—much sweeter and more seductive-sounding than Tsuneko's had ever been.

Now don't get me wrong, but it felt like the tenderest parts of my body were being lightly tickled—you know, like the armpits or the abdomen and so on. And the idea that talking might help me put my thoughts in order seemed convincing, so I said, "Yeah, okay."

My half-brother, obviously no great shakes as a psychiatrist, looked like he wanted to give us his diagnosis: "Growing up watching mothers like both of you had and, though I hate to say it, a sister like that, it wouldn't be unusual for you to turn out to be homosexual. Am I right?

No, no, don't let it worry you. I understand completely."
How could I keep from thinking, "What an idiot!"?

\* \* \*

"Amanda was a totally unknown amateur photographer. She was discovered by Gloria Swanson, the daughter of Amanda's niece. In June 1955, after Amanda's death, she found in the vacation house in Cape Cod that was part of her inheritance from her mother, who had received it from her Aunt Amanda. . . ."

"Hang on for a sec. Cod is a kind of fish, right? Tama *loves* canned cod roe. Be sure and get some for her!"

"In the attic of the vacation house Gloria found an oak chest, and inside it, under some old dresses, a few old cameras, several dozen dry plates, some of which were cracked, several hundred rolls of film of different sizes, and a few thousand faded 5 x 7s. At first she thought the photos had been taken by Amanda's father, Robert Anderson. He was in the import-export business but was also a devoted amateur photographer. A few of his photographs are well known and always included in books on the history of American photography. So she thought these photos were his. But as she examined them, she gradually came to realize that they had been taken by his daughter, Amanda. With the collaboration of a skilled specialist, Gloria made prints. This book contains some of those photos," I explained to Alexandre.

\* \* \*

In a pretentious writing style, Swanson notes that Amanda took a great number of photographs of "a bear, an American Indian, a little girl, a donkey—all sorts of creatures tightly pieced together with the delicate precision of a Japanese inlaid wooden box"; bizarre "fragments of a somewhat grotesque pagan nightmare"; pornographic shots from "an immodest utopia," "fantastical and at the same time nauseating" photographs. It would be inappropriate to publish these in a collection, she says, but she does include just one of the very mildest specimens.

It was a very tame kind of photograph showing a naked man with a headless chicken in his hand, and a naked twelve- or thirteen-year-old girl with blond hair holding a donkey's head in her arms and licking one of its eyeballs with her protruding tongue. It's nothing special, really, except for its overly sharp focus, which, in my view, is typical of Amanda Anderson's photography. This abnormally—one might almost say insanely—sharp focus makes one feel queasy.

The photographs of the country house in Cape Cod from Amanda's girlhood, from around the mid-1890s in Gloria's estimate, remind Gloria of the novels of Henry James. I disagree. The house is a simple two-story white structure built in the period of Henry James, with large windows facing the sea, a spacious veranda and a gable roof. Arranged cozily on the veranda are a white wicker table, chairs, and a sofa. All in all, just the type of house that would appeal to upper-class Americans. But—how shall I put it?—there is no sign of Jamesian characters there.

Apparently Amanda took photos only for ten years, from the age of seven or eight until she was seventeen or eighteen, and then for one or two years in her fifties. The works from her fifties, though, aren't included in the book for the reasons explained above; the ones that are included are all from that first decade. One of the characteristics of these early photographs is that there are hardly any people in them.

The photograph of the white house with large

windows facing the sea must have been taken on board a boat, judging by another photo of the same house shot from an angle and the distance between the shoreline and the house. In the center of the photo is the white house—a simple composition like a child's drawing of a house. The two big windows facing the veranda, the four rectangular windows on the second story, and the small circular window of the attic right under the gable roof are all open so wide that one can see inside the rooms with a crisp clarity, as if peeping into a dollhouse.

At first, I thought it might be a composite photograph. If so, the technique was amazing. But inside each room everything was sharply in focus, even the bed in the room upstairs and the vase with chrysanthemums or roses on the bedside table. It was incredible—and eerie. In the living room, downstairs, one could even clearly see a young maid in a white lace cap and apron and a dark dress holding a newspaper and some letters in her hands.

"I don't know about the pornography of her later period because I've never seen any, but even this photo of a white house is a work of fantasy," I said, handing Alexandre a magnifying glass and showing him the photo. It's understandable that he wasn't as impressed as I was, but since he's easily bored by anything, his response became lukewarm about halfway through my explanation. "Sounds interesting," he said. "You were able to write the script for that porn flick I was in, so maybe you should, like, give up photography and become a critic or a writer or something." Then, looking into the fridge, he asked Fuyuhiko and me, "Gentlemen, would you be happy with a plain omelette, some cold chicken, a salad, and bread?"

* * *

As he ate his omelette, Fuyuhiko looked over the collection of Amanda Anderson's photographs. He seemed considerably calmer than when he'd first arrived, and he proceeded to give us the benefit of the truly stupid reflections of a fifth-rate psychiatrist: "These photographs with no human being in them . . . They're not landscape shots of mountains, the ocean, or fields but photos of places like a vacation home in Cape Cod, or a street in New York, or Coney Island—places normally filled with people. And yet there's no one. That's, well, a little sick, I'd have to say. Seems rather like depersonalization. And then there's the extreme sharpness of the focus—that's worrying too."

His remarks irritated me, but on he went. "Still, these photos are fascinatin'. You know, the director Ridley Scott, who made *Alien*, also made a film called *Blade Runner*, and that was fascinatin' too." Obviously, he was one of those people from Kansai with a bad ear for language who *think* they're speaking standard Japanese but then slip into that Kansai accent of theirs. (The ones who purposely emphasize their accent are even worse, of course.) Well, anyway, he had begun talking with that sort of accent.

"*Blade Runner* is actually a very interestin' film from the viewpoint of my research project. Have you fellows seen it? Isn't it great? It's far more interestin' than the original novel by Philip K. Dick. But these photos by Amanda Anderson are equally interestin'. I suppose it's really *somethin'* to get a copy of this book." (All those dropped *g*'s!) This last was said quite wistfully.

Well, something inside me snapped (which happens very rarely with me), and I shouted something fairly meaningless at him: "Hey, you! You may think you're gonna walk off with this book in place of the mother you think you've been deprived of, but that's not gonna happen!"

"Oh no, I wouldn't dream of doin' that," Fuyuhiko

answered. "But I was wonderin'—I know it's a very precious book, but when you've finished your essay, I was wonderin' if you would mind lettin' me borrow it for just a little while?"

I was so annoyed that I went out, leaving my half-eaten omelette on the plate. The rain had stopped some time before, and I noticed a woman wearing a strange black hat with a black veil, who had just come out of the front door of my landlord's house across the garden and was talking with my landlady in a loud voice. And damn it all if it wasn't my mother!

"So, you see, that's the story, and I'll make sure that Natsuyuki pays the rent he owes you right away!" said Mother cheerfully, knowing that she was going to receive her late husband's insurance money. Catching sight of me, she called out, "Oh, hello there! He's in, isn't he?" mentioning the name of the son whose existence she had forgotten for so many years. I myself had found out about the situation only because the brother of Fuyuhiko's father happened to be an executive at the company where I used to work, and he told me.

"I've decided to give half of the insurance money to Fuyuhiko. You wouldn't mind, would you? After all, you've had me with you all this time, and there'll always be another chance to go to New York." She added that she wouldn't be able to pay for my trip to New York from the other half of the insurance money that she herself would be getting, "because, you know, I have to save for my old age."

"Tōdō was quite a good-looking man with an aristocratic face, so I guess Fuyuhiko must be rather handsome too. You, unfortunately, take after Kobayashi," she said with a frown, referring to *my* father. Then: "How's this mourning dress? It's only a prêt-à-porter, but I got a Givenchy! You know, my size hasn't changed since I was young, so ready-made dresses fit me just fine—no need for alterations!" she said proudly.

I had become so used to this kind of thing since my childhood that I was neither surprised nor overcome by an urge to strangle this crazy mother of mine. I just felt enough was enough and told her, "He's in my room. Why don't you go in and introduce yourself?"

"All right—it'll be mother and son meeting for the first time in thirty years. I'm so nervous!" Her high heels clacking noisily, she made her way across the garden stepping stones.

\* \* \*

Finding it all too much, I went out to Mejiro Avenue only to realize that I didn't have a yen on me. It seemed way too much trouble to go back home to get some money, so after a moment's thought, I decided to borrow five thousand yen from the man at the secondhand bookshop and then went to have some saké at a nearby watering hole.

As I drank, I began to feel that everything was just too much trouble. As for Amanda Anderson's photography, why not let Fuyuhiko write an academic paper or whatever? After emptying a third glass of sake, and while eating some deep-fried fresh-water crabs whose shells made my mouth and tongue prickle, I recalled the smile of Anna Karina gradually forming as a subtle gray shadow emerged in the fixer there in the darkroom where I was enlarging the photos of her taken by some film critic twenty years before. The precise moment when what had been a mere shadow floating in grayish water took on form, giving me a pleasure that almost brought a sigh—that memory vividly came back to me, even though I hadn't taken the photos myself. Then I realized that all I wanted was to see the hundreds of Amanda Anderson's photos that had not yet been printed in that same way—floating in the fixer in some darkroom. I had no need to write anything about Amanda's photographs.

Feeling a tap on my shoulder, I turned around to find Alexandre—how on earth did he know where I was?— wearing my raincoat as if it were his own and standing there saying, "You rushed out with no money." Then smiling brightly, he said, "Wasn't there an actress named Gloria Swanson? She was an ugly duckling."

"Why?" I asked out of politeness.

"Because she was the glory of a swan's son!" he answered, which made me wonder if Alexandre might possibly be a rather clever guy, rather than a good-looking but dumb hybrid delinquent who'd scored the lowest grade in English in junior high. Meanwhile, Alex had an idea: "Let's get money out of your mom or Fuyuhiko and go to New York together! I bet Gloria Swanson's still around. She must be an old witch by now. You should just write to Philomela Press, and if that doesn't work, you can look for the house in Cape Cod. By the way, I brought the book along so that guy couldn't steal it. You're too soft, you know, Natsuyuki," he admonished.

FOUR

# Wandering Soul

Given how they had settled in at my apartment—I'm
not talking about Tama, of course—if I wanted to list
the benefits to me in the situation, there was the fact
that Fuyuhiko had a reasonable amount of money so we
could live on that for a while, and also that he was a fairly
tidy, orderly sort of guy. And Alexandre, semi-delinquent
though he was, actually liked to clean. Even though it
wasn't his own apartment and he would be staying only
for a short while, he didn't like things to be messy or dirty.
The two of them set to work cleaning my rooms. What
with the fluff balls and cat hair and whatnot, it had gotten
to look like a pigsty, but now the windows and the toilet
and the kitchen fan were all gleaming. I guess those were
the benefits to me.

It's easy to write a line about the windows and the
toilet and the kitchen fan, but the dirt of everyday life
accumulates in other places, spots that should be made
clean and orderly. Of course, if one doesn't think in
terms of "should," there's nothing wrong with leaving
things just as they are. But if you do feel like cleaning, the possibilities are endless. Alexandre, wearing only
blue shorts with red piping, his honey-colored body hair
shining with sweat where the sunlight hit it, busied himself cleaning the bathroom tiles with a tortoise-shaped
scrub brush.

"You're wonderfully industrious!" I said.

He answered, "Well, my 'pillow-geisha' granny in
Fukagawa was real strict the way she raised me. 'This lad'll
be a handsome man like Uzaemon or Egawa Ureo before

long,' she'd say, the clammy old bag. She's kicked the bucket by now, but she used to work her ass off servicing her clients back then. It wouldn't have been a tiny *asari* clam she had; it'd have been a lot bigger, her having used it so much. That's the way it is with the women in our family." This last was said in a voice intended for Fuyuhiko to overhear. Then he made a point of asking me, "How about it? Tsuneko's cunt must've been reeeal loose, eh?"

Fuyuhiko glared at Alexandre with a none-too-happy look on his face, and I had to explain to him, born and bred in Kyoto as he was, about Fukagawa geisha—how they were usually called "*haori* geisha" because they wore a short *haori* coat over their kimono when they entertained clients, in a way that seemed stylish. And how Fukagawa was also known in the old days for the *asari* clams that were found in the nearby waters, and how the broiled flesh of *asari* and spring onions served on a bed of rice is called a "Fukagawa-style lunch-in-a-bowl." So Fukagawa suggests *asari*, and that's why Alexandre called his Fukagawa geisha grandmother a "clammy old bag."

As I went on explaining, the bathroom tiles, which had taken on a dull rose color from the hot water "fur," started to regain their original smooth luster; the cloudiness vanished from the stainless steel drain board thanks to the metallic, soap-laced Brillo pad from America; the tufts of pubic hair that had been drifting over the bathroom floor along with balls of cotton fluff were no more; the floors that had been buried in books and newspapers showed themselves again; and the dishes and silverware—everything, in fact—took on a new look.

\* \* \*

"Gee, thanks for cleaning up like this. It must have

been quite a job. Would you like a cup of tea? Or a beer?" I tried to make myself as agreeable as possible, but I couldn't settle down and relax, somehow.

Tama, who'd seemed to want to escape from the racket of cleaning and had drifted out of the apartment for a walk, now drifted back in. She began sniffing at the tatami and floors, which were giving off a strong smell of cleanser. Round and round she went, unable to settle down. Fuyuhiko ordered me to "take in the futons that we put out to air in the sunlight, if you don't mind, before we have our tea."

As Alexandre and I beat the dust out of the futons prior to taking them in, my senile old landlord came by, greeting Alexandre loudly in English. As always, he mistook me for his grandson, and advised me that making friends with a foreigner was the best way to learn English conversation. "Get in as much practice as you can. And take your foreign friend—is he an American?—out for sukiyaki or tempura. Here." He pressed three thousand yen into my hand. Fuyuhiko, who was watching all this from the veranda, had a funny look on his face as he gazed at us.

"What was that all about? That old guy . . . How much did he give you?" asked Alexandre.

"Three thousand yen. He's my landlord, and has gotten senile. He thinks I'm his grandson. I don't know what to do about it."

"What a stingy old geezer! You can't treat a foreigner to sukiyaki or tempura on three thousand yen!"

"He thinks prices are the same now as they were twenty years ago."

"Go tell him this isn't enough!"

"I'm going to return the money to his wife."

"Why bother doing that? Why not just keep it?"

"I can't do that."

"Tsk. Mr. Upright, even though you haven't got an income."

Alexandre tossed the futon he had been holding into the room, and I went to return the money to the landlord's wife.

"Oh, I *am* sorry! He keeps mistaking you for our grandson in high school. Oh, wait just a moment, please." She went back into the house and came out with a box of *kasutera* sponge cake. "Have some of this with your friend. Someone sent it to us, but it's really too much for us to eat by ourselves. You know, your mother was saying the other day that your elder brother is visiting from Kyoto just now. Your mother must have gone through some very hard times in the past. I'm so glad everything is working out well now."

The other night when Mother visited me wearing her black Givenchy suit and black hat and veil, all decked out like some tragic heroine, she must have gone on and on about her troubles to the landlady, who found herself weeping tears of sympathy at such a sad story. Realizing this, I was chagrined but managed a vague reply. Mother must have taken in Fuyuhiko completely too, with him believing every word of her heart-wrenching confession.

"When you met Mother the other day, did you actually fall for everything she said?" I asked him later.

"Not everythin', no. But I understood her. She's a kind of seductress, you know. Of course, callin' your own mother a femme fatale is a little problematic, but . . ."

"You think she's a femme fatale? She's just easy, that's all."

He gave a kind of low moan. "After Dad found himself deserted by his wife and with a child on his hands, he lived like an invalid in a villa in Arashiyama for two or three years. A young woman from Wakasa came to look after him durin' that time. I think my grandparents intentionally sent this 'carnal country type,' could we say? anyway, this amply endowed girl to serve as Dad's maid."

Alexandre put his oar in: "When your dad was taking a bath, that well-endowed girl would've hitched the hem of her skirt up to the elastic bottoms of her panties and shown off her thighs as she washed his back. Then your dad would have gotten excited and forgotten all about his runaway wife. That must have been the idea."

"Right. And that's what actually happened. He regretted what he did that day, but ended up marryin' the girl. Treated her like a servant till his death, though. Her name was Suzuko, but he called her O-Suzu and acted all high and mighty. It was really ugly. He was bedridden for a few years before he died, and O-Suzu had to do everythin' for him."

Listening to this, I felt that I'd read something very similar in a novel. What was it now? The father had deserted his family and was living in Kyoto with a woman who'd worked in a bar somewhere, and his son comes to see him on some business or other and is served sukiyaki. Then after a while, news comes that his father has died, and he goes back to the house in Kyoto and is almost seduced by his late father's lover. The night before the funeral, as he stays up all night in accordance with custom, she whispers, "Aren't you cold?" Then she drapes a coat over his shoulders, which she then proceeds to rub gently with both hands. "You're so like your father," she says, and it sounds kind of suggestive and sexy the way she says it. He remembers how when they lived in Tokyo his father always made a point of saying that he was making Kantō-style sukiyaki, but he had his Kansai mistress make it in Kansai style. Now whose novel was that?

I was distracted by these pointless thoughts. And where on earth had I read that novel? There aren't any novels like that here, I thought, looking at my near-empty bookshelves. As I idly read the titles on the spines of the books, I saw the title *Truth and Falsehood*. Oh yes, a long time ago a certain woman poet had stayed in my apartment for a week or ten days, together with Lily, her diarrhea-prone orange tabby. She'd found this book at a used bookstore on Mejiro Avenue and thought the title "clever," so she'd brought it back and started to read it. She gave up midway, though. "This guy's novel is so old-fashioned. I much prefer Mishima Yukio!" she remarked. The story I'd remembered was in this collection, I recalled, and taking it off the shelf and examining it, I saw to my relief that it was so. That ignorant woman poet had written a poem entitled "Truth and Falsehood" that was published in *Modern Poetry Notes* or possibly in one of those special issues of *Eureka* featuring experimental poems. I remembered also how I had read it standing in the aisle of some bookstore. When I asked Fuyuhiko whether he had made it with O-Suzu, this half -brother of mine answered with a shocked look, in a stronger than usual Kansai accent, "How could you think such a thin'?" Alexandre laughed out loud and commented, "You look as if he's put his finger on it! I just hope O-Suzu didn't look like Tsuneko. That would be sooo clichéd."

\* \* \*

While the two of them took turns showering, I was to make our dinner. It didn't take much "making"—only about fifteen minutes of work: I wrapped three broiled chicken legs I'd bought at the local shop in aluminum foil and heated them up in the toaster-oven. I also made a salad from canned corn and scallops from which the water had been drained off, plus thinly sliced cucumbers with a little salt sprinkled on them. When the cucumbers had got a little tender, I squeezed out the excess water and added a mayonnaise dressing. I poured the remaining liquid from the canned scallops into a can of Campbell's New England Clam Chowder along with some milk, then added some thinly sliced mushrooms sautéed in butter and heated the whole thing up. I also made a lettuce and onion salad. As I said, it only took about fifteen minutes, but by the time I was done, I was all tuckered out and didn't have much of an appetite. Besides, the sound of the two of them busily munching away at their lettuce got on my nerves.

"Those green salads they sell at McDonald's and Kentucky Fried Chicken are really awful, aren't they? They keep the veggies in water so they'll look good, but it takes away every bit of flavor. Not even a rabbit would want to eat those veggies! They're really 'rabbit rejects.' Hey, Tama baby, do you know what 'kitty reject' means? It's salted salmon. . . ."

Alexandre jabbered on, returning once again to his most recent favorite topic: how he'd actually seen a guy with two penises. I was so sick of it!

"What's the matter? You're not eating much. If you're not going to eat that roast chicken, cut it into small pieces and give it to Tama. No, don't give it to her like that, dummy! You've gotta cut it up fine—really fine! How would you like it if someone tossed you a whole pork leg and said 'Eat it!'? Given her size, it's the same damn thing! How can anybody be so insensitive?"

"Well, but cats have a feral side to them, you know. They catch chickens and pigeons and the like. Why, there's a stray in my neighborhood in Kyoto that's a real hunter. When I was a kid I read Ishii Momoko's *Tom of the Hill*—children's literature, I guess you'd call it, or boys' fiction, or . . . Anyway, there's this cat named Tom, and he captures a squirrel in the hills and eats it up—all but the tail. They probably aren't much good, those tails—just bones and fur."

"What the hell are you talking about? Don't put strays and semi-feral cats in the same category with our Tama! She's a cultured city kitty, after all. You can't blame her if she can't handle a whole chicken leg as is!" Alexandre was good and angry. "Hey, Natsuyuki, looks like you've finished eating and have some time on your hands. Chop some of that chicken up for Tama." He was giving me the same order for the second time. "Now, at that public bath just behind Mont Blanc in Jiyūgaoka . . ." He was launching into the story of the man with two penises again.

"Look, as I said before, you're mistaking his testicles for a penis."

"Absolutely not!" he insisted.

I was getting irritated and shot back, "Just what are you trying to say? You must know the old saying 'Heaven never gives two gifts to one and the same person.'"

Reacting to my tone of voice, he said, "I don't know why you get so upset. Oh, wait a sec, I see now. You're envious of the guy! My point was just that there are lots of weird people in this world, that's all."

\* \* \*

Fuyuhiko didn't seem to be much of a drinker. He'd only had a little beer, but his face was bright red. "Gosh, it feels like I'm back in school again." He leaned his head back against the bookcase with too much force, as it turned out, since the books stacked at the edge of the third shelf thudded to the floor at the moment of impact. What a slob! He looked really drunk, but observing him, I could see that he was deftly trying to extract information from Alexandre.

Now me, I don't see what's so great about Tsuneko, but, as they say, "Some prefer *tade*." So, I don't get it, and I certainly don't share it, but there you are. Speaking of *tade*, or smartweed, when you put some of it marinated in vinegar on salt-roasted horse mackerel, the grassy, bitter flavor's really great. After Ma left home—I learned about this later—my dad, Kobayashi, had an affair with a girl working in his office. In those days they called them BGs (Business Girls) rather than OLs (Office Ladies), like now.

Anyway, this unfortunate young BG had an older brother who was a yakuza who'd killed somebody and gone to prison for it, and Dad was really attracted to this modest, unfortunate young thing. At his wit's end, he took me, his little boy, by the hand and went in search of his wife, checking every place he thought she might have gone. Now where was it? Maybe at the home of a former classmate of Ma's during her girls' school days? There was this big garden with a pond where I fed bread to the carp. When Dad and I left, they gave us some *tade* from the garden, and we went and bought horse mackerel at the fishmonger's, set up a little brazier in our garden, and grilled the fish. Then Dad crushed some of the *tade*, added a little vinegar, and that was our supper!

It was during summer vacation, a really hot day, and, what with Ma gone, there wasn't even any chilled barley tea in our fridge so I was drinking ice water. Dad said, "How about a glass, son?" And I had a glass of beer.

"Wow, that tastes good!" I said.

"Have some more," Dad suggested, so I did, finding it cold and a little bitter and delicious. Well, I got drunk and fell asleep, and the next day I had a bad hangover with a splitting headache and diarrhea. I just lay there, feeling utterly miserable, and Grandma, who'd come over to see how we were doing, was indignant: How could she have left her precious grandchild in the hands of a man who was so low as to let a small child drink alcohol to the point of having a hangover? She brought some bicarbonate of soda from the kitchen and made me drink it. Then she whisked me away to her house, and somehow it was settled that I would live with Grandma for a month, or a year—or was it two or three years?

Then when Ma got remarried to the real estate agent, I went to live with them. There were two sons a lot older than I was and a newborn infant. ("Your little sister!") At that rate, I felt that there might be another sibling named Akihiko ["Autumn Lad"] or Haruki ["Spring Tree"] hidden away somewhere as well. Anyhow, I don't think I've tasted *tade* vinaigrette since then.

My dad may have been troubled in his own way by what had happened, but he seemed to be in a pretty good mood then. Or maybe it would be safer to say that I don't remember that day all that clearly. I do remember he was there that evening, but it was like something from a dream. Dad talked on: "Tsutayo"—that's my mother's name—"was born in the year of the tiger, though it wasn't the strongest type of tiger year. You know, they say snake meat is much less oily than you'd think. Tastes like horse mackerel, apparently. Now if Mommy and Daddy decide to live apart, which do you want to be with?" That's what he asked, and it's a hard question to put to a little kid. I couldn't help thinking that only a really dumb guy would ask his kid a thing like that.

What with thoughts like that swirling through my mind, somehow everything became too much of a bother. The feeling that there was nothing I really wanted to do crept up from the tips of my toes. As I lay stretched out on the floor, I reached up to the bookshelf and took down a green packet of photographic paper and gazed at the quarter-size photos of Anna Karina that I'd enlarged. Fuyuhiko, who was also stretched out looking a bit dazed, asked, "Can I take a look at the photos?"

"Sure," I said, passing them to him.

"Say, isn't this, oh, you know—Anna Karina?"

*Wow, this guy sees movies other than* Blade Runner! I thought to myself. "Yup, it's her."

"These are fine photos, really fine." Just like when he'd seen *Amanda Anderson: Photography and Life*, he gave me the benefit of his views, as if he *knew what photography was all about*. Not only that, he pointed out how the photographer praises the subject, and gazes at him or her through the small anonymous device known as a camera, and how the subject returns in the direction of the film the fascinated gaze of the photographer, who is at once anonymous and possessed of a particular physical body. Thus, the subject Anna Karina is radiant with light, including the reflections from the mirror behind her. Hearing this critique, I was almost dumbstruck with awe at Fuyuhiko's display of knowledge. But then he started to talk about what a neurasthenic female patient of his once told him.

First there was the story of how Anna Karina left Godard and the house, or perhaps it was an apartment, where they had been living, and of how Godard, in tears, went in search of her. Then there was the story of how Anna Karina later claimed that even when Godard slept, he kept one eye open. Well, when you search for a lover who's left you, you'd certainly run around looking with tears in your eyes, wouldn't you? The city of Paris that Godard knew so well must have looked different, cold and distant; all the little streets and the grand avenues like radiant flower gardens; all the buildings, the Seine, all the bridges would seem like things seen for the first time, like alien things, huge and enveloped in hard cold silence, wouldn't they? His body must have been swollen with suffering and his senses dulled. Yet the noises of the street would have pierced the tingling skin of his whole body like fragments of glass or metal, or like thorns. They must have truly seemed love's "sting of death": a mourning of the spirit, the sense that he had begun to lose something truly unrecoverable, a lump of sadness that choked him, something hard that he could not possibly swallow. He crossed the Pont Neuf and the Mirabeau Bridge, wandering the streets, and all the while the image of Anna occupied his mind and heart. He had premonitions of the death of the love that was now turning into hatred and despair.

I felt I had to say something in response to this account of Fuyuhiko's, so I made some comments that seemed unlikely fully to get through to him: "Yeah, but in *Laughter in the Dark*, based on Nabokov's *Camera Obscura* and directed by Tony Richardson, Anna Karina looked really fat. She was no good at all. The character Margot is an usherette at a movie house and has a clean-shaven neckline a la Louise Brooks, but Anna Karina comes out with long, flowing hair. That Tony Richardson's got no talent! He grabbed Evelyn Waugh's *The Loved One* for himself when Buñuel was planning to direct it. And he should have left *Camera Obscura* for Joseph Losey to do."

Fuyuhiko kept nodding in an admiring sort of way as he listened. "It's extraordinary that you think so, too," he said, and I was afraid he was going to continue with "Us bein' brothers and all, even though we were raised apart." But no: "Yes, you know, the girl I was treatin' said the same thin', exactly the same thin'. . . . Oh, I get it now. You and she must have been readin' the same movie reviews." He'd explained it satisfactorily to himself. It made me mad, but I didn't say anything and was thinking that I'd like to meet this former neurasthenic patient of Fuyuhiko's. You don't come across somebody who thinks just like you do that often, after all—though I might be wrong about that. Maybe it's not so unusual, in fact. And how could I ever get to meet this neurasthenic young woman who seemed to spend all her time talking about movies, anyway?

"She was quite a pretty girl. She should be at college here in Tokyo by now, I suppose," Fuyuhiko continued, and I was suddenly made oddly aware of my own extreme loneliness.

Tama ate up all the shredded chicken, then for the first time in a while washed her face with her front paws in leisurely fashion, carefully licked the fur all over her body, and, though it was too early for fleas, nibbled away at herself here and there. She wetted her fur with saliva so that it stuck close to her body, and when it dried, her coat was soft and fluffy. She'd turned into quite a beautiful cat. Alexandre contentedly stroked her, murmuring, "Yes, yes—

'On a red plum tree
set out to dry
just-washed kitty!'"

He cradled her in his arms, supporting her back, and as he gently rocked the "mother," whose reddish, swollen, fresh, mammalian nipples could be seen amidst her white fur, he kept repeating, "Good kitty, good kitty, my Tama's a good kitty, my good little Tama" When he got tired of that, he put Tama into the closet where the cardboard box with her newborn kittens was. "Okay, now give your babies some milk! Cats and Godard—just the same," Alex concluded.

"I sent the hospital in Kyoto a notice of absence due to illness this mornin' by special delivery, and even if I am to take a kitten, it's impossible until they've been weaned. Plus, none of my patients has serious symptoms, so there's no harm done if I'm away for a while. And anyway, I'm in no condition to be treatin' patients. Besides, I never did think I was meant to be in clinical practice. So, I think I'll stay here for some time." That was what this madman, totally lacking in common sense, had announced that very morning. He intended to settle right in.

"And what might you mean by that, Alex?" he asked with that prissy pronunciation intellectuals are given to.

Alexandre, for his part, informed us, "Yeah, right now I'm thinking of changing my name to Felix. Alex . . . Felix . . . Which sounds better?" On he went, in a nonchalant way: "Oh yeah, I saw on TV a little while ago this video on cat ecology. There's this town on the seacoast, a really old town with, like, lots of narrow roads going up hills and stone steps and all—like a maze! 'Course there are people living there, but it's just full of stray cats, including house cats. And there's been this rule for centuries that you can't raise dogs there. You know how in the Tokugawa period, there was a time when everybody had to be really polite to dogs—Master Dog, like . . . 'Laws of Compassion,' they called it: Kill a dog, and they'd cut off your head.

"So I figure in this town somebody must've killed a stray dog or something, and ever since, they've thought having dogs is bad luck. Or something like that, anyway. With no dogs around, it's cat heaven! And lots of people come from all over to dump their cats in this town. Well, in the video the hero is this really big black-and-white male cat that belongs to some family. During mating season, he goes crazy for a calico female, but, even though she seems interested in him—like in the phrase 'I'd fall at a single touch'—whenever black-and-white brings his nose close enough to sniff under her tail, she scratches him with one of her front paws—like, over and over!

"But black-and-white won't give up and chases the calico up hills and stairways and on top of roofs all over town. It's like a labyrinth, though, or the Kasbah, and he loses sight of her. Suddenly the calico's nowhere to be seen. He calls out to her in front of her family's house, but she doesn't appear. Well, black-and-white frantically searches the town for her, calling out with that terrible sound cats make when they're in rut—rrrawr, rrrawr. He's really frantic and excited and goes up and down the hills and back and forth through the narrow alleys. He forgets about grooming his coat, and it gets all dirty and ratty-looking. A sad, love-crazed cat! Pitiful . . . Really touching . . .

"Now what was it? You know—the flick we saw together in Takadanobaba the other day. Oh yeah, *Hécate*, by Daniel Schmid. That's it. Remember the guy who was in it? His girlfriend disappears, and he runs around like a lunatic looking for her, and ends up killing somebody. Yeah, the actor was Bernard Giraudeau. Right. It was just like that, and when I saw the flick, I cried 'cause I remembered black-and-white.

"But then, in the video, this white female cat shows up and seduces black-and-white, who's still looking for the calico. She lifts her tail and shows him she's all hot down there. She's seedy-looking—small and thin, not at all sexy. But she chases after black-and-white and shows him her ass. 'Course black-and-white ignores her, won't have anything to do with her. He's mad for the calico. His eyes have this empty look as he lets out that miserable cry of his. And yet, in the end, he screws the white one. He mounts her, bites the scruff of her neck, works his hips back and forth and 'Meeeoww!'—he comes. Yup, he does!"

"How's that the same as Godard?" I put in.

"I just wanted to point out that cats are basically like human beings," answered Alexandre. "Even the maddest love becomes just a memory as time passes," he continued, laughing like some cunning old crone.

Fuyuhiko was silent, with a gloomy look on his face. I realized he might suspect that Alexandre was one of Tsuneko's young lovers rather than her little brother. I myself had heard a rumor to that effect at one time, and the cameraman who made the porn video that Alexandre starred in had insisted that was so all along. "But what would be the point of them lying and saying they're brother and sister?" I defended a more orthodox view of their relationship, but the cameraman was having none of it, I recalled. And Fuyuhiko, as a man in love, would be all the more prone to jealous doubts, since "fear creates its own bogeymen." It was all making me most uncomfortable. Fuyuhiko took from his bag two kinds of medicine, gulped them down, and then proceeded to spread his futon and lie down on it. "Excuse me. I'm goin' to go to bed a little early tonight." Alexandre turned to me with an expression of disgust on his face, and I gave a deep sigh.

\* \* \*

When would I be able to go to America? And even if I got to meet Gloria Swanson, the daughter of Amanda's niece and the author of *Amanda Anderson: Photography and Life*, in Boston, there was no guarantee whatsoever that she would first show me Amanda's unpublished rolls of film and then give me permission to make prints from them.

Plus, I hadn't yet determined whether Philomela Press was still in Boston or not. I wondered too whether in fact they had ever existed—those strange pornographic photos that Swanson describes as "a bear, an American Indian, a little girl, a donkey . . . all sorts of creatures are tightly packed together with the delicate precision of a Japanese inlaid wooden box"; "fragments of a somewhat grotesque, pagan nightmare"; pornographic shots from "an immodest utopia," "fantastical and at the same time nauseating photographs." Nearly baseless anxieties of this sort started to rise within me. And I wondered, too, if, having seen these alleged photographs, which would no doubt have an impact on an actual viewer, my own reaction would be anything other than a feeling of nausea.

When I tried saying in broken English something to

the effect that "I am very proud to have the honor of introducing the photographs of Amanda Anderson to Japan for
the first time," I felt embarrassed to death.

Then, too, it gave me a headache to recall my mother's
words of the previous day: "I still feel young! I'm sure I can
manage another one or two men in the near future, but
when I *do* really get old, I want to live with you, son!"

Thinking of this and that, I began to drowse, only to
be awakened by the sound of someone sobbing. I was
sure it must be Fuyuhiko, and I couldn't help flinching at
the thought. But, contrary to expectations, it was Alexandre who was sobbing. I figured if I just pretended to
be asleep, he would eventually stop. But he kept sniffling
away and fumbling around in the dark for the box of
tissues and finally noisily blew his nose. "What's wrong?"
I called out.

"Oh, sorry. Did I wake you up?" he answered with a
little laugh, his teeth showing white in the darkness for a
moment. "I woke in the dark and was looking up at the
ceiling, and then I thought about how I'll die all alone, and
it, like, scared me."

Of course, everybody—I'm talking about children
here—has experienced that, so it's not that I didn't understand his feelings, but I felt a bit hesitant. I don't know
how old Alexandre really is, and he's of mixed blood,
probably with a G.I. father. And he's got no academic qual-
ifications, no job, and no fixed address. So, when he says
things like "The streets were my school," like a character
from Genet's *Our Lady of the Flowers*, I flinch back a bit at
his cheap, would-be-intellectual pose.

But what I'm talking about now is something different—an annoying innocence, shall I call it? Now this is a
really trite sort of idea, but if Alexandre were a woman,
one of us would snuggle up in the other's futon in a case
like this. The one who's crying might snuggle up against

the one who's going to offer comfort, or it might be the opposite—it doesn't matter much. And the hand that's stroking the other's back would slowly move down toward the buttocks, and meanwhile that person's lips would kiss away the tears from the other person's moist eyelids, and before you knew it, you'd be having sex. That would be the not-so-innocent consequence.

But I decided that it was Fuyuhiko's professional responsibility to ease the victim of "ontological anxiety" whom I found sobbing beside me, and not mine. I felt like waking Fuyuhiko up as he lay snoring there on his futon, having taken two kinds of tranquilizers before bedtime. But then I realized that I'd have to get involved in the whole thing and lose a night's sleep myself, so I changed my mind.

I lit a cigarette and put it to Alexandre's lips, then poured some Rémy Martin that I'd brought from Mother's place into a glass and gave it to him. I'd been keeping it in a desk drawer, not because I'm stingy but because I didn't see why I should give it to those two. I couldn't very well console Alexandre the way I had Tama when she was suffering from postpartum depression. (Tama: "Am I going to die? Am I? Meow? Meow?" She kept crying sorrowfully in a hoarse, gloomy voice. Me: "You're a nice cat, Tama, so you won't die!") So, as we talked on, I told him the story of a pilot that I happened to recall just then, though I thought at the time that it might not be quite the thing for the occasion. We all told a variety of stories that day, as it turned out.

"It's about these pilots flying for a postal service through the mountains of South America. It's dangerous work: The planes are pieces of junk, and the weather in the mountains is always changing, with fog sometimes and thunderstorms at others. It's pretty rough work, and you never know when an accident will happen. Well, one time one of the pilots fails in an attempt to land in the fog. They're able to pull him out of the burning plane, but he's in such bad shape that there seems no chance he'll survive. So they put him on a stretcher and carry him to a room in the pilots' lodge. The guy knows he's gonna die, and he says to his buddies, 'Everybody dies alone. That's the way it is. I'd like you guys to leave the room now.' One of his buddies puts a cigarette between the lips of the dying guy and gives a nod, and everybody leaves."

"I'm just a gigolo," said Alexandre, lying on his belly as he sipped at the cognac and hiding his eyes, wet and messy, behind a pair of sunglasses with a black celluloid frame. "I've been an actor and a bartender and a performer, but I've never made a living at anything. So you see, all that beauty and moral purpose that the pilots who risk their lives have—that's got nothing to do with me! They're like brave old elephants, I guess you'd say. But I'm not."

"Yeah, yeah, I see. Sorry about that," I said, pulling the quilt up over my head and adding, "Watch that cigarette, okay?"

\* \* \*

I was awakened by the sound of Alexandre, up early that morning, talking loudly in the garden with my landlady. I opened one eye and glanced at the clock by my pillow. It was only seven-thirty. Beyond Alexandre's empty futon, Fuyuhiko could be seen reading a newspaper.

"Well, good morning!" he said, noticing me there with my one open eye. "I just couldn't get to sleep last night. . . . "

*Can't a guy even go to bed and get up when he wants to, in his own room?* I thought, my head aching. *I'm not getting up!* And I pulled the quilt over my head, intending to go back to sleep if only to spite the two of them. But then Alexandre came back and started to make breakfast in the kitchen. It smelled like miso soup and dried horse mackerel and *natto* fermented soybeans, plus the vegetables pickled in rice bran paste that the landlady had given us.

"Oh, but will a foreign gentleman like something like this, I wonder."

Seeing how doubtful the old lady was, Alexandre made a point of answering in broken Japanese, "Yes, yes, me like Japanese pickles veeerrry much! Me not mind smell. *Fromage*—how you say that? Oh, oh—cheese! Same, same."

And so it went. As the two of them sat at my kitchen table, Alexandre said, "This is the basis of Japan's food culture—this combination of foods centering on rice!"

Fuyuhiko disagreed: "Not at all. This combination is a rather special one within the context of Japan's breakfast culture. There are regions where they eat rice gruel cooked in tea with pickled plums and other types of pickled vegetables . And they eat various types of flour in certain areas. There were even places where they used to eat barnyard and foxtail millet. This business of 'white rice equals Japan' is a very ideological notion." Good Lord, they were starting to debate first thing in the morning! I hadn't had anything much to eat the previous night, and I was one hungry guy. So what could I do but get up and have breakfast with the two of them?

\* \* \*

I'd promised to write twenty pages about Amanda Anderson in a special issue on "Unknown Artists" in some magazine for intellectuals at the rate of a thousand yen per page, and today was the deadline. But I didn't feel like giving them even a glimpse of Amanda for such a shit-small sum of money. Who gives a damn about the "promise"? If the editor started kvetching, I'd just shout, "Bastard! Don't think you can buy a man's insights for a mere twenty thousand yen!" Of course, I'm not sure I'd actually say that when the time came. But I had some ready cash on hand, and what would be the point of introducing the photos of the "unknown artist" Amanda Anderson in that magazine anyway?

"It sounds really interesting. I'd definitely like to include these photos," said the idiot editor; but I didn't have the original prints, and you couldn't expect something printed from a copy of a photo in an anthology to be much good. Why, it would be a kind of sacrilege to use such lousy copies of photographs by Amanda, whose focus was always so sharp—maniacally so. When I asked myself why I'd agreed to do the article in the first place, it came down to "Poverty dulls the mind."

As I went over all this in my head, I was chewing a pickled mini-turnip with my molars. I'd had some root canal work done on one of them. There was a filling where the cavity had been, and the problem tooth had then been fitted with a metal cap. One part of the tooth that was now especially thin and hollowed out broke off. It brushed against my tongue, mixed in with the mini-turnip I'd been chewing on. I used my tongue to separate the chip of tooth from the mini-turnip, and, after swallowing the pickle, spat the piece of tooth out onto the palm of my hand. It was much smaller than it had seemed when in my mouth—a thin, dirty-brownish fragment of tooth.

As I held it in my fingers and examined it, I felt a sense of loss of a sort that I hadn't experienced when I'd had a tooth pulled or my appendix taken out. People have this really profound sense of loss when they lose a part of their body, apparently, especially in the case of women, if it's their ovaries or uterus or a breast. But you hear of people who feel the same way about a lung or a part of the stomach or the pancreas. I guess a human body that's missing one of its major organs seems really terrible. "Ah, is this how death begins, then?" Suddenly I was talking to myself.

The sleep-tangled futons were still spread out on the tatami, while from the open window the deep pink of the double cherry blossoms, half open, was visible in the garden. The scent of the blossoms was carried into our room on the breeze, and Alexandre was repeating to Fuyuhiko the landlady's instructions for cherry blossom tea, which he had heard shortly before.

"Wow, double cherries are so nice! I wonder if I should change my name to Haruki ['Spring Tree']," remarked Alexandre as he drank the cherry blossom tea from last year, which the landlady had given us. "*Your Name Is . . .*" answered Fuyuhiko, and Alexandre, not getting the reference to an old radio play with a hero named Haruki, just nodded vaguely. Then (I wondered when they had agreed on this) Alexandre said, "Auntie won't know where Tsuneko is right now either, but if you're going to go see her, I'll come along, since I've got something else to talk to her about. I guess you should keep on looking for Tsuneko to your heart's content. But I don't have any money on me, so you pay the train fare to Auntie's for both of us, okay?"

"Oh yes, of course." And so it went.

# FIVE

# Evanescence

"I love drinking cherry blossom tea, just pouring hot water over salted cherry blossoms," said Alexandre, yawning. "There's something *aromous* about the way the pale pink flower sways in the hot water," he added.

"What's 'aromous'? Is it Tokyo dialect?" asked Fuyuhiko.

"Dialect? What are you talking about? Aromous is aromous."

"Does it mean something like aromatic?"

"Don't be stupid. Don't you understand Japanese?"

I heard what they were saying, but I just couldn't be bothered to chime in and help them out. I only thought what a stupid fellow Fuyuhiko was. Given the context and the description of "the pale pink flower swaying in the hot water," like a glass paperweight with a flower and water sealed within, "aromous"—regardless of whatever caused Alexandre to make this error in the first place—must clearly mean "amorous" here. I could have corrected him, but I thought it would be even more fun to watch Fuyuhiko, who still couldn't get it and looked really puzzled, than to embarrass Alexandre. So I just averted my gaze and tried not to laugh.

"I guess 'Haruki,' 'Sprin' Tree,' signifies a cherry tree," said Fuyuhiko, eager to change the subject.

To which Alexandre innocently responded, "Then do Natsuki and Fuyuki refer to some specific summer and winter trees?"

Fuyuhiko, who seemed at a loss for an answer, gave a kind of groan, and then managed to reply, "Well, I suppose those are more—how shall I say?—abstract images. Parents name their son Fuyuki, wishin' him to stand bravely on harsh terrain and in difficult circumstances. Natsuki, 'Summer Tree,' on the other hand, represents the parents' wish for their son's vitality and prosperity."

Alexandre just said, "Oh, yeah?" and started explaining to me how to make salted cherry blossoms.

"You got all those double cherry blossoms out there. Why don't you give it a try? The old landlady was saying that cherry blossom tea is the ultimate Japanese-style prop for celebrating a happy occasion. You probably don't have too many happy occasions, but anyway, for cherry blossom tea, you've got to use double cherry blossoms. With the ordinary kind, the flowers would just go limp from the salt.

"Apparently it's best to use flowers that are seventy percent open. You need fifty grams of salt for two hundred grams of them. Put a light weight on top, and in two or three days discard the water that's seeped out. Now this is an important point that I myself didn't know till she told me, but you know how cherry blossom tea has a slightly sour taste? Those trademark salted cherry blossoms on top of Kimuraya Bakery's red bean buns taste a little sour, right? That sourness doesn't come from the cherry blossoms themselves. And it's not because of fermentation. It's different from the ripe pickles made from bok choy Chinese cabbage. It's because after getting rid of the water, you add about half a cup of red plum vinegar and let it stand for a week or so, and then put the flowers on a flat basket in the shade. When they're dry, you sprinkle a little salt on them and put them in jars or something to preserve them. Isn't it great to view this year's cherry blossoms while drinking cherry blossom tea from last year? 'Where are the cherry blossoms of yesteryear?' Why, they're right here!"

"Indeed," said Fuyuhiko, "and the same could be said

about Villon's line 'Where are the snows of yesteryear?' They're here, dammed up and flowin' through the tap, and with the cherry blossoms of yesteryear floatin' right there on top."

"Yeah, yeah, right. And she said it's really nice when you're making a boxed lunch or something to mix a little plum vinegar in with cooked rice and then make rice balls with one or two salted cherry blossoms on top of each rice ball. Only you shouldn't eat the cherry blossoms like you do with red bean buns. You've got to save them till later because it's, like, elegant to have them as cherry blossom tea or instead of the usual broth after the meal."

"Oh, indeed?" Fuyuhiko said again.

I was so sleepy after being woken up by the two of them early that morning that I suggested, "If you guys are going to go out, I wish you'd go out now. Then I can get a little more shut-eye."

"You sleep all the time, Natsuyuki—more than a cat does!"

"Never mind about that—just go," I said, slipping into one of the futons that were still spread out on the floor.

"What'll we do about supper?" Alexandre asked. "Oh, well, we won't be all that long, so I suppose we can think about it after we get back." I ignored his question, pulled the quilt over my head, curled up, and closed my eyes to get to sleep again.

\* \* \*

It was around ten when the two finally went out, and when I woke from my nap, it was two in the afternoon. It had only been a four-hour nap, and I felt like sleeping longer. But as I lay there looking up at the cloudy, gray sky through the shiny-clean window pane, I remembered the molar that had been chipped that morning when I was eating the pickled turnips. And though it wasn't exactly because of this chipped molar, somehow I felt as though my whole body was sinking into a lethargy that made me sigh—it was like air heavy with gray-white moisture. It seemed worst around my hip area. The numbing heaviness was really depressing.

As I scratched my belly, which had gotten warm and a bit itchy among all those quilts, my fingertips touched some pubic hair. And though there was nothing special about it, the touch of this coarse and kinky hair provided a kind of comfort—a little like the feeling you get when you stroke a cat along its back, though usually pubic hair is much coarser than a cat's fur. After a while, my fingers began to play with my penis in its usual, non-erect state, which is much smoother and more sensitive than a cat's fur. This was not, of course, masturbation; it was more like a cat grooming itself by licking its coat, and as with cats, this "grooming" comforts us.

It's quite true. There's this really weird young man, a student-type I sometimes see in a coffee shop in Mejiro. One glance tells you he's seriously neurotic or has some other abnormality. He picks his nose, rolls his snot into a ball, and after taking a really good look at it, he flips the ball of snot—as if by a sudden impulse—at a young female customer who is deep in conversation with someone. Or if he's not doing that, he puts a hand in one pocket of his baggy trousers under the table—he must have cut a hole in the pocket—and plays with his penis. You can tell for sure that he isn't masturbating. No, without doubt it's a kind of grooming that calms him down.

Sure, it's not a pleasant sight. He seems really weird, since both nose-picking and penis-grooming are basically unconscious, solitary actions. When reading a book, for example, we often find ourselves picking our nose or playing with our penis—admittedly, they're rather infantile actions—so there's nothing really new in his doing these things, but normally we don't do them in a coffee shop. So when you see someone do such things, the reaction would be something like what I witnessed some time ago: a group of four girls were busy gossiping about their friends. One of them noticed what the young man was doing and, with a strange look on her face, nudged the girl sitting next to her and whispered something to her. Then that girl briefly glanced at the young man, blushed, and quickly looked away with an ugly, sulky look on her face.

The other two girls, who were sitting with their backs to the young penis-groomer, had no idea what was going on, so they asked loudly, "Hey, what's wrong?" "What is it?" The first two girls gave them a "Hush!" sort of look, and the four put their heads together over the table and had a whispered conversation. Then, "Oh, my God!" "You're kidding!" "Yuck!" "He must be crazy!" "How grotesque!" They made so much noise that the staff and customers in the shop looked their way. The girls ducked their heads and giggled, "Oh, ick! Everybody's looking at us!"

The young penis-groomer gave them only the briefest of glances and stayed as cool as a cucumber. "Let's go, girls!" "Yes, let's!" They pulled out their purses, big and small, split the check for their cake-and-coffee sets and blueberry yogurt and, still giggling, pushed through the exit. Then, peering back at the man in question through the shop window and exchanging comments all the while, they walked toward the intersection.

This is the way the average girl would react. Men would probably just pretend not to have noticed. As I indulged in such vague thoughts, I got tired of touching my penis and rolled over to lie face down without the pillow. I rubbed my oily face against the sheet, getting some of the oily sweat off, and then lay still. I became aware of something sticking to my lips, so I rubbed my hand against them and then returned to the same position. Something was still sticking to my lips.

I raised my head to see what it was and found a wrinkle in the sheet right at the spot my lower lip had been touching. The sensation of being tickled lightly on the lip was somewhat *aromous*, if you like. But when I realized what it was, sleepiness crept up from the base of my neck, and just as I was falling back to sleep, a girl who seemed to be a classmate of the two girls next door started making a racket, trying to open the locked glass door between their rooms and the garden.

"Anybody hoooome?" she shouted into the obviously empty apartment, and to top it all off, she then pulled open the glass door to my apartment and, even though I was in bed, asked, "Are your next-door neighbors out?" What was she thinking?

I was so annoyed that I brusquely answered, "I don't know." Then the girl, with her hair in an Osaki Midori–style bob—"in other words, it looked as if she'd chopped away at her hair herself with a pair of scissors," I later explained to "Fuyuhiko the Psychiatrist," who was so in love with writing research papers. He gave his usual canned opinion: "When women cut their hair by themselves on the spur of the moment, it's a kind of self-punishment." What a bore!

Anyway, this young woman, who was wearing a strange blackish dress, noticed Tama, who was asleep with her kitten on the veranda, and cried out, "Goodness me! Tama, what a' y'all doin' here?" I'm not sure if those were her exact words, but at any rate, she said something very close to that to Tama in a Kansai accent, which took me by surprise.

"Do you know this cat?" Before I could stop myself, I asked that of this girl whom I had never seen before.

"It's not exactly that I know *this* cat," she answered, "but I used to have a cat called Tama who looked just like this one. So for a moment I felt as if my Tama, who disappeared, had found a home here."

While we were chatting, the students from next door came home. "Oh, you're here!" They apologized for bothering me, and all three went on to the girls' apartment next door. But soon the girl I hadn't met before came back on her own:.

"You know, my Tama loved chasing after a little ball that I made for her from aluminum foil. After playing with it for a while, she would toddle back to me with the ball in her mouth, meowing and looking at me as if she was asking me to throw it again. She did this over and over, fetching the ball and bringing it back in her mouth until she got tired of the game." Then, totally uninterested in my reaction to her story, she went back next door.

After about an hour had passed, this time my neighbor Momoko came along, speaking in a very low voice: "Say, Natsuyuki . . ."

"What?"

"That girl who was here—don't you think she's a little strange? She's in the same seminar with us, but she just came over today without any warning and shows no signs of going home. I don't know how to handle things like this. What should I do?"

"Well, that's *your* problem. I have problems of my own—*two* strange visitors, and a cat as well!"

"How can I get her to go home?" Momoko went on, though I could hardly be expected to come up with an answer to that. Sitting on the veranda and lazily leaning over to stroke Tama's back, she said, "She seems to like you a lot, so how about coming over to our apartment in a while and taking her out somewhere and then just sort of leaving her in front of the station or wherever?" That was a cheeky request.

"You know, Momoko, in a metropolis like New York

or Tokyo, you can't live by being so dependent on other people. You girls should be able to get rid of this one crazy little chick between the two of you." As I gave this ser-monette, Momoko's aunt passed by just outside our hedge carrying a plastic shopping bag from Peacock Supermarket and a big budget pack of five boxes of Scottie tissues.

"As usual, you people seem to have nothing much to do," she said, and came in. Momoko's aunt is a novelist who lives nearby, and when I was still working as a pho-tographer for the company that later went bankrupt, we happened to go to Akita together on an assignment for a magazine. We sort of hit it off for some reason, and since we lived in the same area, we often visited each other.

When Momoko explained the situation, her aunt stated decisively, "You've got to handle this kind of thing on your own. Just ask her to leave." And then, lighting a cigarette and taking a puff, she said, "Rita Hayworth's dead, you know. She had Alzheimer's. They say they found the virus for it in a sheep's brain. So it's an illness of sheep as well. Well, sheep aren't very bright now, are they? They've got this very dumb look on their faces. So if they get Alzheimer's, how do they end up looking, I wonder." She sighed, and continued: "After becoming ill, Rita Hay-worth apparently wandered around the garden muttering, 'I'm Gilda, I'm Gilda.'"

"What's a gilda?" asked Momoko. The novelist explained that Rita Hayworth had been married to Orson Welles, to an Arab prince, and to a boxer, and then elab-orated on the evil charm of the scene in *Gilda* in which Rita Hayworth sings a song, accompanying herself on a guitar. "And as for sheep," she continued, "I'll tell you what happened to a sheep."

I could guess what this childish novelist would say, so I went ahead: "I know. The sheep goes to school, right?"

She looked very frustrated and added, "That's right.

It wanders around the classroom baaing, 'I'm Mary's little lamb, I'm Mary's little lamb.'" Then, with a jaunty "Bye" she went home.

Momoko, totally unimpressed, said with a deep sigh, "That joke was just as unfunny as the gags in those manga by Akatsuka Fujio after he began to go downhill."

When I told all this to Alexandre later, he announced with pleasure (though whether it was true or not, I can't say): "A long time ago, when I was still a teenager, I used to work in a transvestite bar in Akasaka. I wore a long red wig and a Gilda costume, and I sang and played the guitar. But isn't that cute? Imagine, a sheep with Alzheimer's— now that's cute!"

\* \* \*

Meanwhile, Fuyuhiko had returned from Kamei, where he had gone with Alexandre to see Alexandre and Tsuneko's aunt in order to get information about Tsuneko. "Alexandre isn't his real name," Fuyuhiko reported. "His aunt kept callin' him Kanemitchan. So it's Kanemitsu— probably written with the characters for 'combine' and 'light.'"

But the very existence of this aunt seemed to have convinced Fuyuhiko that Tsuneko and Kanemitsu a.k.a. Alexandre were at least a real half-sister/half-brother pair. He said that he had requested the aunt to tell Tsuneko, if she had the chance, that he desperately wanted her to contact him. Like a wanderer in love, he sighed and leaned back against the bookcase with his eyes closed, apparently indulging in memories of Tsuneko.

I made a point of reminding him of our own mother. "Tsuneko seems pretty much the same type of woman Ma was, don't you think? Your father's younger brother happened to be an executive at the company I worked for. He stopped me one day and said, 'Your mother was once married to my older brother, and they had a son called Fuyuhiko.' But when I asked Ma if the name Tōdō meant anything to her, she said, 'Tōdō? I know a dodo is an extinct bird, but Tōdō?' She'd completely forgotten everything. Though when I explained, she did manage to recall it.

"Now, I'm not suggesting that all women are like that, and meddling in someone else's love affair is the last thing I want to do. But don't you think she's a lot like Ma— Tsuneko, I mean? Why do you want to find her? No matter how long you stay here, I doubt she'll ever contact me, and it's unlikely she'll ring to ask how Tama is."

When I said this, Fuyuhiko insisted that when he went to her apartment in Yoyogi Hachiman, Tsuneko was showing a lot of affection for Tama, and that Tama, too, was really attached to her. Unusually for him, he spoke without using any analytical jargon, but I found it all too much and fell silent.

I decided instead to try to think of various excuses for not writing the essay on Amanda Anderson that I was supposed to contribute to a special issue on "Unknown Artists" for a certain magazine. The deadline was upon me, and obviously, as a professional writer, it would be unacceptable to back out on something you'd agreed to do just before the deadline, and it would certainly cause trouble for the people involved. But, after all, I wasn't a professional writer—just an unemployed photographer.

So it wouldn't be like failing to carry out a photographic assignment; I could be excused for not writing the essay I had agreed to write. That was the selfish justification I came up with. And besides, once Amanda Anderson's photographs were shown in mere reproductions from the original book, most of the charm of her photography would be lost. Yet it would be awfully strange not to include any photos in an essay on her photography. And above all—though I should have realized this much earlier on—there was absolutely nothing that I wanted to say about her.

"Oh, but . . ." The young editor on the other end of the line might be at a loss for words, but I would just repeat, "I can't write it. I don't want to write it," and then maintain an autistic silence on my end of the line until the other party realized there was nothing for it but to give up. This strategy would certainly reflect badly on both my character and my intelligence, which sort of reminded me of how, in my childhood, my mother used to criticize me in a disgusted way: "You manage to be both indecisive and terribly stubborn as well!" That was the sort of comment she would make when, for example, there were two things available and someone told me to choose whichever I liked. It took me the longest time to make up my mind.

In this and similar situations, my new real estate agent "dad" would try to smooth things over by saying, "There, there—Natsuyuki is a very prudent young man." But being prudent is one thing and being indecisive is another. I must admit that what Ma said more correctly describes my personality to this day. So despite what I'd said to Momoko from next door, I couldn't get rid of my own unwanted guests or the cat, and was tossing around various ideas as to how to get away with not writing what I had agreed to write. I wasn't all that different from that young man in the coffee shop who made snot balls and, hand in pocket, played with his penis. These quite depressing thoughts might well have been triggered by Fuyuhiko suddenly turning up in my apartment. Surely anyone would be depressed to see a man obsessed with the ridiculously old-fashioned motif of searching for a lover who was both lost—or missing—and unfaithful.

Thinking of all this, I felt thirsty and decided to make

myself some tea, which I could hardly do without asking Fuyuhiko if he wanted some too. So I asked this half-
brother of mine, who replied in a faint voice, "Oh yes,
actually I *am* thirsty." Drinking the cup of tea with milk
I made for him, Fuyuhiko seemed still lost in thought,
though at least he showed enough consideration to pour
some milk into Tama's saucer.

The girls next door had apparently succeeded at last
in persuading their unwanted guest to go home. As the
three girls were crossing the garden from the veranda to
the sliding gate at the far end of the hedge, the girl with
the raggedy bobbed hair turned around looking puzzled
for a moment, came quickly toward us and addressed
Fuyuhiko: "I was right. It's you, Doctor! What on earth are
you doing here?"

I thought she'd say that he was the spitting image of
Dr. So-and-so, whom she'd studied under at school a long
time ago, or something like that. But Fuyuhiko immedi-
ately responded in his professional voice, "Oh, Miss Ino,
how have you been? You look very healthy indeed! You're
feeling well, I take it?"

"Yes, thank you, Doctor, I'm fine," Miss Ino said. "I
don't get as upset about thin's as I used to. I think I'm completely recovered; I don't take medicine anymore."

"Oh, that's good news. But if thin's ever get bad again,
give me a rin' any time. I'll write a referral to a doctor in
a hospital here. Oh, by the way, Miss Ino, did you cut
your hair yourself?" He sounded as if he had begun to feel
unsure about her recovery.

"Yes, suddenly I just couldn't stand havin' long hair, so
I cut it myself. Does it look funny?"

"No, no, it's fine. But didn't you have some kind of
problem or other? If you're havin' trouble sleepin' like
before, you should see someone at a clinic here."

From the above exchange, Miss Ino must have guessed

that her doctor thought that she was still unwell, so she insisted again and again that she was feeling just fine and then went home.

The girls from next door came back from the gate at the hedge, heaving deep sighs. After nodding hello to Fuyuhiko, they urged me, in a kind of sign language, to come over to their apartment, as if they wanted to say something confidential. I had to scuff into my sandals and go over to their veranda.

"From what I heard of their conversation, I'm sure your guest is a psychiatrist, right?" whispered Hanako, Momoko's flat-mate. When I said he was, she moaned, "Ohh, I'm so *tired*!" and collapsed on the floor.

"Me too," cried Momoko, collapsing on the floor herself. She waved "See you" to me, so I said, "See you" back, and returned to my room.

"That girl—it's not good, her cuttin' her hair like that," muttered Fuyuhiko as if talking to himself. "It doesn't look good. She appears to be fine, but choppin' away at her hair like that is an act of self-punishment. By the way, she's the young woman I was talkin' about last night—you know, the one who likes movies."

*Oh, that explains it*, I thought. But I also remembered that while listening to him talk about her the previous night, I'd thought of my own lonely way of living and felt somehow like meeting her, which was uncharacteristically sentimental of me, I had to admit. The tea that, due to this unexpected interruption, I had been unable to drink was by now lukewarm and unappealing. But I was so thirsty that I gulped it down and, having nothing to say, silently smoked a cigarette. Then Fuyuhiko suddenly pulled himself up into formal sitting posture:. "I've really imposed on you," he said, "and I thank you for puttin' up with me. I've decided to go home to Kyoto today."

"That's good. Yeah, I guess you'd better," I said.

"Please say good-bye from me to Alexandre and Mother. To be honest, I'm not sure if I'll ever see either of them again, but . . ."

"Yeah, that's right. I envy you. I wish I could ask some-body to tell Ma that I'm not sure if I'll ever see her again," I commented. "She *is* my Ma, and she did take care of me for more than ten years, but if she *weren't* my mother, I'd have absolutely nothing to do with her. We have nothing in common. *You* have no obligation at all since you were, like, abandoned by her when you were a baby. Lucky you!"

"Well, I don't think it's a matter of who was luckier."

"But"—I must have felt so relieved about Fuyuhiko finally deciding to go home that I became somewhat chatty—"what'd you think when you realized that Ma had completely forgotten about you?" I asked. "Actually, I wish she'd forget about me too!"

"She couldn't have totally forgotten everythin' for more than thirty years. To be more precise, when, out of the blue, you asked her about the Tōdō family, she just couldn't remember right away. I think it's probably quite common."

Put that way, I could see that he was right. Hearing Fuyuhiko's brief reply, I realized that I'd been taken in by the romantic fantasy (shall we say?) that my ma had com-pletely forgotten about her own child and his father. And that was because I had unconsciously adopted the myth that no mother could ever forget about her own child.

Fuyuhiko quickly got ready to leave. "If you come to Kyoto, be sure to come and visit me. And please tell Alex-andre that as well. It was an almost absurd coincidence, but I'm glad we met," he said and then left as abruptly as he had come. So, for the first time in quite a while, I was all alone in my apartment, which was unusually clean and tidy. Dazed and taken aback is how I would describe my state.

\* \* \*

For many days after that there was no contact from Alexandre, which was a relief, since it meant he must at last have found another place to stay. And after a series of complicated negotiations, I managed to get away with not writing the essay I was supposed to write on Amanda Anderson.

As for Tama's five kittens, the girls next door found someone to take the one with orange tiger stripes on a white ground. The porn photographer, my former colleague, said, "Actually, my wife has been wanting to get a cat," and took one of the tortoiseshells. The black male kitten with a white nose and white paws went to the old landlady of the Red Plum Lodge, who was particularly fond of its markings. "Oh, this little one looks just like the cartoon character, Norakuro!" she exclaimed. Her husband, our senile old landlord, was against the idea of calling it Nora on the grounds that it was "the name of a woman who leaves her family, so it's no good for a house cat." Nevertheless, the kitten was given the name Nora-chan.

The ikebana master from Ekoda, who was a regular customer at Tsuneko's bar and had, it seemed, been swindled out of several million yen by her on the pretext of pregnancy and childbirth, had earlier agreed to adopt a kitten, and I wanted to take advantage of this commitment and give him *two* kittens, so I told him on the phone, "The kittens are weaned, and it's the right time for adoption. They really are so cute!"

So he said, "Oh, it's quite close if I go by car," and on that same day he came over. This plump, sociable, middle-aged flower arrangement master shook his pinkish head topped by hair kept neatly in place with some sort of oil or pomade. "Oh my! What cute little claws, shiny as pearls! You know, I imagined that since it was Tsuneko's

cat, it must be a Persian or a Himalayan, or perhaps a Siamese or an American shorthair—something of that sort.
But you know, I love this kind of Japanese cat best—they
are *so* cute."

Then, without saying another word about Tsuneko, he
asked, "Do you think you could take photos of my ikebana
school's exhibition? It's going to be held at a department
store in central Tokyo in June." He went on to praise the
double cherry blossoms at Red Plum Lodge and was also
filled with admiration for "this garden with its great variety
of trees." Just then the old landlady dropped in, explaining, "Nora-chan and I'd like to say hello to the papa of the
house his brothers are going to." The master repeated for
her benefit his praise of the beautiful double cherries and
the rich variety of trees in the garden, and while chatting
about this and that, they discovered that my landlady had
taken ikebana lessons from none other than the grandfa-
ther of the Ekoda flower arrangement teacher. They were
all in a twitter over the coincidence.

And then the old lady said, "The kittens you've
adopted, Master, are very sweet indeed, but I must con-
fess I was a fan of Norakuro in the *Boys' Club* magazine
that our son subscribed to, so I fell in love with Nora-chan
here."

"You're right, he's just like Norakuro. You should give
him a collar decorated with stars."

"Yes, indeed! I'll make tiny appliqué stars for it," she
said with a quaint little laugh.

They talked for quite a while, and when it was finally
time for the Ekoda ikebana master to go home, he picked
Tama up saying, "Time to say good-bye, Tama-san." He
even went so far as to take her over, quite unnecessarily,
to the kittens he was taking away with him. In any case,
the two kittens, which had been put inside a towel-lined
cardboard box, were quite unsettled, bristling their fur

and showing their razor-sharp teeth and pink oral cavities as they mew-mewed and meow-meowed. They were safely placed in the passenger seat of the master's white Porsche and off they went. Tama started to cry loudly, looking for her missing five kittens, so the old landlady put the one remaining next to her. "Here's Nora-chan, Tama-san!" But that didn't make up the number, so Tama would sporadically wander around in search of the other kittens. This continued for two or three days, after which she completely forgot about her kittens and returned to her normal self—her ordinary cat life of deep sleep by day and wanderings outside by night.

By then all the double cherry blossoms had gone, and several pale pink and dark red peonies had started to flower. The soil of the flower bed where those peonies were planted was so soft that it must have been quite comfortable, and both Tama and Nora squatted there as if in a trance, doing numbers one and two. This upset the old landlady, who had earlier been remarking that the sight of the big and small black-and-white cats sitting entranced under the pink and crimson peonies was just like a Japanese silk painting.

The old landlord, a former English teacher, somehow got the idea of drawing the cats in his sketchbook, and in general, everything was peaceful. As for myself, I'm not a photographer who specializes in cats, so I had no intention of taking photos of Tama or Nora. Instead, I did some pretty miserable casual work, such as printing yucky nude photos of amateur girl models that the pornographer-photographer had diligently taken. Meanwhile, I waited for the three million yen that, according to my late stepfather's will, I was due to inherit to be transferred into my bank account after the necessary formalities.

My ma's plan to change the beneficiary of the insurance from her late husband's sons from a previous marriage

to me wasn't successful since time had already run out. So
the insurance money, which would have come to one or
two hundred million yen according to Ma's calculations,
vanished. "Dad was careful about things like this, so most
of his fortune was in his company's name, and I got just a
tiny amount. I don't want to lose any of it, since I'll need
it in my old age. I'm wondering if you couldn't give what
you've got to Fuyuhiko," said Ma illogically, while trying
to drive Tama away by blowing cigarette smoke at her, so
that her black Chanel suit wouldn't get any cat hair on it.

"No way!" I said.

"Why not?" she continued. "That's not much to ask.
You were able to work in that publishing company—
though it *did* go bankrupt—purely thanks to Itsuo-san of
the Tōdō family, and he helped you out because I used
to be married to Tōdō. And, you know, this three million
yen inheritance wouldn't have been there either if I hadn't
been married to Dad. You were always with Mommy.
[In fact, she ran out on us when I was very small, and it
was only the summer when my grandma died when I was
in the third grade that she got married to the real estate
agent and decided to take me in.] But Fuyuhiko—oh,
that poor boy! Couldn't you give up that money to help
your mommy atone?" She continued to talk nonsense: "It's
not money you earned by working yourself anyway, and
wouldn't it make you feel better to do something for your
own brother?"

"Not in the slightest."

"Oh, really? Well then, what about giving him half the
amount?"

"I won't give any of it to him, and he wouldn't accept
it in the first place."

"Oh, really?"

"Of course not. How insensitive that would be!"

"Oh, really?"

"If you actually want to do something for him, why don't you leave your money to him?"

"But I won't have anything left. There won't be any."

It went on like this, Ma wanting to look good in Fuyuhiko's eyes while not wanting to use her own money to do so. "Oh well, we might just go to Kyoto, and the three of us can have dinner together—my treat!" she said.

What's this all about? I felt. And who's this aged woman with heavy makeup here in front of me? But, "That sounds okay," I responded in an uninterested way.

"Yes, that might be the thing to do," she finished with a seductive smile. "I'm quite busy now since I've got to plan for the future!" And leaving the scent of her perfume everywhere, she went home. I was exhausted.

\* \* \*

Several days later Alexandre came by without warning.

"What did you do with the kittens?" he asked without bothering with the usual greetings. When I answered, "Every one of them has found a home," Alexandre's response was: "How much do you know about the identity of the people who took them?"

So I said, "How can you, of all people, talk about identity?"

"I'm not talking about the kind of identity the Japanese war orphans left in China want to confirm," he snickered. "You get it, don't you? It's, like, whether they're people with a sense of responsibility toward cats." His preachy tone irritated me even more.

"Hey, Alexandre, what about you and Tsuneko then? Are you people with a sense of responsibility toward cats?"

"You're changing the subject! Tsuneko entrusted Tama to me, and I entrusted her to you 'cause I thought you were a responsible person who'd look after Tama. Have I ditched Tama or let the Health Department kill her? Have I? And just take a look now—Tama seems so happy and satisfied! There're some really irresponsible pet owners. When they find it too troublesome to look after their cats, they take them somewhere far away and just leave them there. And there are even creepy sickos who cut cats with utility knives. So you never know."

"OK, but these people are all fine. They'll take good care of the kittens."

"That's all right then. How have *you* been? You look like you're not doing anything much, as usual, but I've had a terrible time. I stayed with my aunt in Kamei for a while, and one day she invited some people over to play mahjongg, and there was this friend of hers who runs a bar in Ōi. She asked me what I did, so I said I was out of work, and then she went, 'Do you want to work for me?' and I ended up working at her bar in the bar and restaurant district in Ōi for a while.

"It was a real nothing place, with the owner's apartment upstairs and a little three-mat room at the far end of the bar that was unoccupied. 'You can use this room for the time being,' she said. I knew I couldn't stay with you forever, Natsuyuki, and I wanted to earn enough to buy canned food for Tama. So I decided to work there for a while, even though it was such a terrible place. I'm quite a—I hate to sound arrogant, but—good-looking guy." Alexandre explained that the forty-something proprietress of the bar came to his three-mat room after closing time from the very first night he started working there. "Since she came, I had to do it, but my, she was insistent! I got really fed up. I did bear up till the third night, but today I decided to award myself the money in the bar's till as payment for my work as bartender as well as her bed companion. And that's why I'm here! So

I've got some money, though not much, and I thought I'd treat you."

"But that woman is your aunt's friend, isn't she? She'll find out you've run off with her money in no time, and then she'll ring up your aunt and demand the money back, don't you think?"

"You worry too much, Natsuyuki. Besides, I didn't 'run off with her money.' I just took the 'self-declared wages system' one step further."

"Plus, what you did could be regarded as prostitution."

"Well, each of us might have a different view on that, but in any case, you don't have any money, do you? So stop arguing, and let's go out and get something to eat," said Alexandre. "Or is it a bit too early for that?" he concluded, folding a large flat cushion in half and putting it under his head. As he lay there, he stretched to full length the four legs of Tama, who lay asleep beside him, and said with a somewhat sly smile that could be interpreted as smug or simply happy, "Cats are *ya~rakai* (so~ft), don't you think?"

"It's *Ya~raka*, you see? Give me a pen and paper or something."

Using the ballpoint pen and note pad I handed him, Alexandre wrote horizontally in his almost illegible hiragana writing "やーらか" and said contentedly, "It's like this. The two little lines sticking out from the top part of や are the ears, and the つ shape within the letter is the face, and the downstroke is the front paw. The long vowel sign—is the body of the cat, and ら is the right hind leg bent a little, and the main part of か is the cat's bottom and the left hind leg, and the 丶 mark is of course the tail!"

\* \* \*

We went to a Taiwanese restaurant in Takadanobaba

and ordered all sorts of things and ate and drank a lot. "Don't you worry, Natsuyuki. Yesterday was the second Saturday of the month so the bank was closed, which means the take from Friday night was there as well. For a miserable little place, you'll be pleased to know there was two hundred thousand yen! I'll treat you in grand style tonight.

"How's your sex life, by the way? You don't seem to have a girlfriend. It's not my thing to pay for sex with a woman. It's a terrible waste of money, don't you think? But just for tonight, why don't we go to a 'soapland' together? I was a sex slave to that woman for three long nights, so I'm exhausted," said Alexandre.

"Thanks, but no. I'd rather have—I know you'll probably protest, but I'm going to have Tama spayed, so why don't you pay for the operation?" I asked, while placing on a dish the tiny bones from our order of quail and taro stir-fry.

As predicted, Alexandre started to fume. "That's just the egoism of human beings, ignoring the importance of animal life!" He agreed with all his heart with the opinion that I'd mentioned earlier of the professor of sociology at the University of Tokyo, who was also a regular contributor to the *Asahi* newspaper's current affairs columns. "Even if you were to end up killing kittens with your own hands, you would at least be accepting responsibility for their pain as a member of the community of living creatures. Cats don't choose to have that kind of operation— they're disabled just for the sake of human convenience!" he concluded indignantly.

"That's a fine opinion," I said, "but let's take the viewpoint of a female cat." As a matter of fact, in preparation for refuting Alexandre, i.e., the opinion of the professor at the University of Tokyo (needless to say, a man), I had read a reference—an essay that was published in *Kurashi no techō* [Notes for Living] and had been recommended by Momoko's aunt specifically to counter Alexandre. When I said, "Do you know Tomioka Taeko?" Alexandre said no, and when I said, "She's a writer," he asked "Is she a major writer?" "Of course, and she wrote that cats that have kittens grow visibly older and weaker every time they have a litter. Human mothers, too, used to have many, many children, and all their nourishment was sapped by the fetuses and newborns, and the mothers aged prematurely. It's the same with cats: fetuses sapping nourishment and kittens sucking away milk. Every time a mother cat has a litter, she becomes haggard and worn especially in the hip area. Her coat loses its gloss, and she sheds lots of fur as well. Generally she becomes very weak. We're not talking about Tomioka's own cat but about a homeless female in her neighborhood that once came to consult her."

"Did you say a cat came for a consultation?" said Alexandre.

"Yes, that's right. 'I want to have a sterilization operation. What do you think?' she asked. Tomioka Taeko found it a very reasonable question. She told the cat, 'You'd better have it,' and paid her expenses."

"Ummmm," pondered Alexandre with a quail bone in his mouth. "Are you sure it was the cat's free will? The cat said she'd have the operation?" This made the young couple sitting at the next table steal a suspicious glance at him.

"Of course! She's a truly genuine writer. She never writes lies," I said emphatically. "And Tama agreed. I read that essay to her, and she said, 'I'm completely with her. *I* wouldn't like to have kitten after kitten till my body is a wreck.'"

"Is that what Tama said?"

"Yup."

"Well then, we can't help it, can we?"

"Nope."

"How much will it cost?"

"I can check, but twenty or thirty thousand yen, I'd guess."

\* \* \*

That is how Tama came to have an operation at the beginning of summer, before the next mating season started. The vet told me that, though it would be easier and cheaper too to have the ovaries removed, for the health of the cat, because of hormone and other issues, removal of the uterus would be the better option. Exactly how the two methods differ wasn't quite clear to me, but in any case, it sounded convincing enough, so I said, "OK then, I'd like to go for the better one, thanks." I was told not to feed her the night before and to "bring her in after letting her pee that morning." So I put Tama in my camera bag and took her to the pet clinic.

Alexandre was supposed to come along with us, but he didn't turn up even after the agreed time. I knew that might happen, so I carried the bag containing the cat on my own to the veterinary clinic on Mejiro Avenue. Tama had peed before we went there, but the needle scared her, and she peed again. Apart from that, everything went much more easily than expected, though when I saw her lower abdomen wrapped in bandages with her fast asleep, still under the influence of the anesthesia, I found the sight quite pathetic. When we got home, I put her in the cardboard box. After a while she woke up and, unlike human beings, she wanted to move around even straight after the operation, which made me really anxious. But she was as lethargic as any invalid.

With still no word from Alexandre, it was time to have her stitches removed, so I put Tama in the bag again and took her to the clinic. As he removed the bandage, the vet said, "Oh no, poor thing!" I thought for a moment that something had gone wrong with the operation. "Look." He showed me the incision around which, in the shaven area that had been covered by the bandage, black powdery flea droppings were stuck in little clumps. "Operations in summer have this problem. Poor thing. There, there. It was horrible and itchy, wasn't it?" the vet said while wiping away the flea droppings with alcohol-infused cotton balls.

"Meow!" Tama cried, but after the stitches were removed, which must have been quite painful since she cried "Beow," I took her home in the bag again. Jumping out of the bag, Tama raised one of her hind legs and started licking her abdomen in the vicinity of the incision, which must still have had a terrible iodine taste that made her sneeze and wipe away at her mouth with one paw. Then she started to lick her lower belly again very carefully. After a while, as if nothing had happened, she stretched, yawned, and went outside with tail waving.

\* \* \*

A postcard from Alexandre came:

> How is Tama doing? Thanks for everything. I'm in Izu doing some video work that came in suddenly. Give my love to Tama. I'll bring some lobsters back for you. ALEX

I thought I'd go to New York, leaving Tama under the care of the old landlady. The three million yen had been transferred into my bank account, and I was fed up with Mejiro, where I'd been living for six whole years. As for Tama, I hoped things would go all right for her while I was gone.

# SIX

# Balls of Confetti

"Uway masha?" said Alexandre in a loud voice as he entered from the garden.

"Whaat? What's wrong with you?" said I.

"*Pardon, Monsieur, s'il vous plait.*" Alexandre sat down on the veranda. "Uway masha? How's Tama?"

The idiot was trying to speak French, I realized. "What do you mean, *ma chat*? If she's your cat, why don't you just take her off my hands?" I told him.

"Hey, calm down, Natsuyuki. I've brought you some presents—abalone and turbo and horse mackerel, plus fresh wasabi and pickled wasabi, all from Izu! Hang on just a second." He went out beyond the hedge surrounding the garden, where a small, very smart-looking and flashy foreign sports car (What make? I wondered) was parked, said something to the woman with long, straight hair sitting in the front seat (I couldn't see her face from where I was sitting), opened the trunk, and took out a quite large white Styrofoam box. He and the woman had an extended chat. Then she said, "Okay, see you later!" And with that the sports car took off while Alexandre came back to the apartment, his arms loaded with the Styrofoam box and a round package of wasabi pickles balanced on top.

"Where's Tama? She's okay, isn't she? Poor little thing—after such a big operation."

"Not really," I said, responding to "such a big operation."

Alexandre, however, thought I was referring to his question about whether she was okay.

"So where the hell is she? I *told* you not to put her through that unnatural, inhumane sterilization operation.

I didn't want that done, remember! I bet she's not doing well—nose all dry and scaly, fur falling out. That's how it is, isn't it?" He was all worked up.

I was disgusted. "She's eating like a horse, and when she sees one of the neighborhood dogs, she snarls, jumps at it, and bites. She's probably out bullying one of the dogs right now."

"Oh yeah? She always was a brave little cat. Right from the start she had this—what should I say?—*wild* side to her. Usually she's calm and gentle like a pretty girl from a good family, but . . ." He nodded with great satisfaction. "I got lots of seafood in Izu. Let's make sashimi and have everybody over for a meal! Too bad Fuyuhiko isn't here. Anyway, let's invite the two 'dish girls' next door and the lady novelist, and make a real party of it!"

I asked him what he meant by "dish girls," an expression new to me.

"You don't know much, do you? No culture!" he snickered. "It means they're, like, shallow down there." I didn't catch the last couple of words, and thought he said just "shallow."

"What about you, then? I'd say you're a 'dish boy.'"

Alexandre laughed good-naturedly. "But I don't have a cunt, you know. No culture at all! Those two girlies next door? Their asses are so thin you can bet they're shallow down there too."

"Oh, I see. Sure. . . ." I laughed, wondering if he meant that as a criticism of the two. "Well, anyway, I've gotta go to Nakano now."

"Nakano?! You're going to Sun Plaza? Is there a concert or something?"

"No, it's work—work."

"Work? You? That's unusual. What kind of work?"

"Well, this photographer I know was injured in a car accident, and I'm standing in for him—a kind of pinch hitter. I'm going to take photos of some writer or other. Three usable shots, at fifteen thousand yen a pop, they said."

"Is that, like, low or high as a fee?"

"It's standard, I think."

"Yeah?"

"Anyway, I go there, take a few shots, and come right back. Shouldn't take more than three hours. So while I'm gone, why don't you prepare the sashimi, send the 'dish girls' off to buy the essentials, and basically get everything ready for the party?"

"Oh, listen to Mister High-and-Mighty! Can't be helped. Okay, I'll do it."

Alexandre went to invite the girls next door to the party. "Wow! Sounds kinda swanky!" They were already whooping it up a bit. I called the lady novelist, inviting her to come at such-and-such a time.

"Oh, yes, I'll be right over! I'll just stop by at Tanakaya to pick up something to drink." It sounded as if she was going to take off as soon as she put the phone down. I explained that it was going to be at such-and-such a time, so could she please come in about four hours?

"I know she looks a little dense, but Momoko's family runs a small inn, and she learned to cook while she was still a child. She knows how to prepare abalone and turbo and horse mackerel sashimi for sure, so feel free to make use of her today!" She sounded quite enthusiastic. Then, in an even more enthusiastic tone she said, "Really? You're going to take photos of *him*?"

"Yes. Have you ever read any of his novels?"

"Now, I'm neither a character in nor the narrator of Proust's *The Captive*, so I mustn't say anything too harsh. Even so, I can quote the line that goes 'That could have been written by a pig!'" She snickered a bit.

"Did Proust really write as abusively as that?"

"Sure he did. It's fun to do!" the lady novelist replied.

Her view of my job was that fifteen thousand yen per shot was not bad, pig or not. "Besides, you wouldn't be taking photos of the guy's writing, so why not?"

I was just about to leave with the equipment I'd borrowed from a friend the day before when Momoko and Hanako waved goodbye to me as they got on their bikes. "We were talking to Alex, and we decided to get some sea urchin and salmon roe so we can have sushi later. So we're going to bike to Minofuji and do some shopping!"

Alexandre said that he was going to borrow a small dining table from the landlady and then asked me in a low voice, "Hey, Natsuyuki, you sure you got train fare?" He shoved a five-thousand-yen bill into the pocket of my jeans. "Here, take this." Then he sort of stroked my balls through the jeans, continuing, "My ma had this Korean lover who ran a pachinko parlor. He always said 'a thousand-yen check.' Imagine that—'check'! Well, anyway, see you later," he said, laughing.

*　*　*

The novelist was a guy of around fifty, with a garden-variety three-day beard living in an ordinary ready-built house. I don't know about his writings, but he didn't *look* like a pig, at least. I rang the bell, which resulted in a weak "ding-dong," and we had a brief exchange on the interphone.

I never lock my own front door, so naturally I tried his doorknob, planning to let myself in, but it was locked tight. Soon I had the feeling I was being observed through the little fish-eye lens in the door, and then I could hear the door being unlocked. The door opened to reveal a nondescript man carefully dressed in a white Lacoste polo shirt, beige pleated chino pants, and green socks. He ushered me into a kind of guest parlor, or something close to that, off the entrance. I offered my card, saying the usual "It's a pleasure to meet you," and he made the standard response "The pleasure is mine."

Then the novelist boiled water in a siphon coffee maker and brought out cups and saucers. Just as he was about to put in the ground coffee, he discovered that the can was empty. He was quite flustered. "Oh no! I always buy only a little at a time since it loses its aroma so easily. I didn't realize I was out of coffee!"

"Oh, don't bother about coffee," I said good-naturedly. Then I told him that if you put the fresh ground coffee you've bought at the store into a tightly sealed can and put that into the freezer compartment of your fridge, it keeps its aroma for quite a while. I took enough photos to produce two usable shots of him in the room we were in, and the remaining shot I took of him standing on a nearby pedestrian overpass with a group of high-rise build- ings over which the sun was setting in the background. This was at his request, and he changed "costumes" for it and wore sneakers and a linen jacket. "I really dug that wrinkled linen jacket that Mickey Rourke wore in *Angel Heart*," he explained. As I looked at him through the bor- rowed Hasselblad, I realized that was why he had made a point of having a three-day growth.

"Oh, that's great. Just like that. This'll be good. I wish I had color film." Then I said, "Oh, yeah, how about put- ting these on? I think they'll look super on you." I handed him a pair of Wellington-type dark green sunglasses, and went so far as to say, "Let's do it Mickey Rourke-style. It'll be great!" It was only too easy to get the writer to pose as dramatically as Mishima had done in *Ordeal by Roses*.

"When you take photos of people, you engage in all kinds of small talk. Before working with this novelist, I'd taken photos of discussions between a literary critic

and an associate professor, also as a pinch-hitter photographer," I explained as I chewed away at the abalone
sashimi. "Oh, this really smells of the sea, doesn't it? And
abalone steak is great, too. Well, the critic was a really
smooth guy, with just the right amount of vulgarity to
him. He'd do well at a place like Mitsui or Marubeni as a
department head on the fast track. And he'd be great for,
say, Toshiba Machine."

At this the lady novelist snickered, commenting, "Oh,
he thinks he's too good for that sort of thing!"

Tama, smelling the seafood, had rushed home from
the landlady's together with her kitten, Norakuro. They
stood there with ears perked, eyes wide open, whiskers atremble with anticipation, tails erect and swishing
back and forth, noses furrowed, and pink, moist, rather
fierce-looking mouths open, emitting loud mews.

"Now be careful," the lady novelist advised. "You
mustn't give abalone or turbo to the cats. If they eat things
like that, they become ill and unable even to stand, so you
mustn't give them any. The chopped raw horse mackerel
will be fine for them." Emphasizing her point, she turned
toward Momoko and Alexandre as they worked at their
preparations for the meal. Then she said to the cats, "I'm
not being stingy. They're really bad for you!"

"So this associate professor had these big uncouth-look-
ing fingers covered with stiff hairs, yet he used his hands in
a very delicate sort of way."

"Just like Tokitō Kensaku!" exclaimed the lady novelist and Momoko in unison.

Alexandre asked, as usual, "Who's that?"

Hanako, looking very clever, answered, "They say he's
really Shiga Naoya."

Alexandre was outraged. "Don't you go talking about
things I don't understand when you're eating abalone and
turbo and horse mackerel and fresh wasabi and such—all

bought with the money I got from showing my body in a porn video!"

"Sorry, Alex," I said, and then drank a little of the Chateau Somewhere-or-other wine that the lady novelist had bought on sale for twenty six hundred yen. Then I told them how the novelist whose photos I'd been taking had said that he found it erotic the way the tulip figures on pachinko screens opened their petals when you scored.

The lady novelist turned away with a cool look and remarked, "I told you he was piggish."

"But why are the tulips on pachinko screens erotic?" Momoko and Hanako wanted to know. Their question seemed purposeful somehow.

"How should I know?" I answered. Alexandre was disgusted with the lady novelist. "Why are you talking like some middle school girl that's never had sex? And you, pretending to be an artist! And I bet the guy was having a little fun with you, Natsuyuki—you looking so young and all. He tells you how the tulip opens up as the ball goes in, like you're some kind of super-innocent kid who'd turn red as a boiled shrimp when he heard that."

The lady novelist said with an earnest look, "But you know, we live in a world where, if there's a young man in a novel with the name Tamao [Jewel- or Ballboy], critics can say 'a symbolically erotic name for this character' and be taken seriously!"

"You mean, like, the guy's balls or something?" asked Alexandre. "So what about my Tama? She hasn't got a uterus anymore, but she's still a female!"

"Yes," the lady novelist said. "Some critics can't seem to distinguish between testicles and a penis. Just as some novelists can't seem to distinguish among a uterus, ovaries, and a vagina."

By now Tama and Norakuro were sound asleep in a

corner of the room, and the lady novelist (whom everyone was now starting to call "Auntie," like Momoko, who was in fact her niece), living up, or down, to her new appellation of "Auntie," had placed an elbow on a doubled-over cushion right near the sleeping cats and reclined there yawning frequently. Tama emitted a soundless but most objectionable fart as she slept, which hit "Auntie" full in the face. She gave a sour look without moving an inch, complaining that "Tama's farts are awful, really awful!" and then fell at once into a deep sleep.

"She looks like she wants to say 'I'm as good as any cat at sleeping in total peace, sufficient to myself in the depths of this sweet slumber.' Could that be possible?"

"Looking at her now, it seems a wonder she manages to make a living as a novelist."

We chattered meaninglessly on. Alexandre was working away with a toothpick at a turbo cooked in the shell and guzzling barley *shochu* spirits. "She was talking about people not knowing the difference between testicles and a penis. Well, *I* didn't know the difference between *neko-irazu* rat poison and a *nezumi-irazu* rat-proof cupboard," he was saying with a thoughtful expression on his face. Then the phone rang.

It was Fuyuhiko, now back in Kyoto. "Sorry to have imposed on you like that the other day and taken advantage of your kindness." Then, after a pause: "'Life is stranger than fiction,' they say, and it's really true."

"I think it's 'Fact is stranger than fiction,' actually," I put in.

"Yes," he said, at a loss for words, but seemingly unwilling to admit his mistake. "I suppose, strictly speaking, 'fact' is the right word, but what shocked me about my recent experiences was not so much 'facts' as 'events.' I'd have to say that life is not so much a series of facts as it is a series, or non-series, of events." Then, careful to say that it wasn't his own patients he was talking about, he gave two or three clinical examples.

"*Neko-irazu* is poisoned food used to kill rats, isn't it?"

"Not poisoned food—the poison itself."

"Oh. Well then, what's *nezumi-irazu?*"

"These special cupboards . . ."

"For dishes and things?"

"For dishes and for food. You don't want rats to get at that stuff, so they make these really strong cupboards that rats can't get into. That's what the old folks say."

"But if it's so rats *can't* get in, shouldn't it be *nezumi-irezu*—'not letting rats in'?" asked Hanako.

"But that would give too much autonomous subjectivity to the cupboard," Momoko countered. "You always do things like that. Even with rice-bran pickles. Instead of saying 'ripe pickles,' like everybody else, you say 'ripe pickled.'"

"That's right! And that's why the neutral word *nezumi-irazu*—rats don't enter—is better," Alexandre concluded, "though my grandma and her friends said *nezumirazu.*"

"Yeah, but in my family Mom and Dad both said 'ripe pickled,'" Hanako objected.

Alexandre and Momoko said in chorus, "Your parents are a little strange."

"Now take this 'fact' business. For example, you and I are half-brothers. That's a fact. But our *knowin'* that is, I'd say, an event or happenin'. It *happened* that way. What I wanted to say was that what happened was stranger than fiction. Here in Kyoto, I saw that movie *Hécate* by Daniel Schmid that you and Alex were talkin' about. I'd say that film wasn't about facts but a story about how events are purified until they become facts."

"So why didn't you get the difference between *neko-irazu* and *nezumirazu?*"

"What?"

"No—I was talking to somebody here."

"Do you have a guest there?"

"No, never mind. It's just Alexandre."

"Oh, I see. You know, I'd like to talk to him too, afterward."

"Okay."

"Yeah, but if I don't explain about *nezumirazu* to these girls who've never heard of it, the conversation can't move ahead! Who's that you're talking to? Ohh. Fuyuhiko. Hell, is he getting all weepy on us again? Just tell him Tsuneko's dead, and the baby along with her."

"Say, Fuyuhiko, did you call because you wanted to talk about fact and fiction?"

"Well, I guess I got sidetracked. I'm not callin' about that but about your essay on the photography of Anderson. I suppose you've finished it by now, but just yesterday I got a letter from a grad student who's studyin' in Paris sayin' that right now the works of Amanda Anderson are bein' talked about a lot over there. A photography magazine called *Zoom* just had a special issue on her, introducin' her unpublished porn photos."

"Really?" My voice sounded funny, even to my own ears—hoarse and maybe a little trembly. My face may have paled a bit, too.

Alexandre and the girls, rather alarmed, stopped their chatter, and he asked, "What's wrong? Did something happen?" I shook my head no.

"He says he sent the magazine by separate post, so I suppose it'll arrive soon. The contents bein' what they are, I doubt you could get it at a Japanese bookstore, so I'll send it on to you as soon as I get it. Anyway, this Swanson woman, the daughter of Amanda's niece, apparently married a Frenchman and is livin' in France now, and she's the one who decided on publishin' the porn photos. "The

Flower Garland as Other" is the title of the accompanyin'
essay by Tournier. Have you heard of him?"

"Oh, I see," I answered. "Thanks for letting me know."

"Not at all. But for sure, you're the first one to introduce the photos of Amanda Anderson in Japan! And you'll
be able to see those porn shots of hers that you've been so
curious about for the first time! I've written to the Parisian
publisher and asked them to send you a copy of the magazine by international express mail as soon as it comes out.
I asked them to send me the bill. So I'm sure you'll be the
first person in Japan to see those photos!"

"So what?" I felt like asking. But this guy was talking
like this out of goodwill, and how could he be expected to
know that I wanted to see Amanda Anderson's photos in
the darkroom, as a professional darkroom technician? So
what would be the point of talking to him that way? One's
hopes—should I say?—or dreams are so easily—how shall
I put it?—not betrayed exactly, and not really over, either,
and not destroyed, just simply cut off. And maybe there
weren't even any dreams or hopes to begin with.

"Well, I look forward to seeing them."

"I'm sure you do. And I hope they're all you were
expectin' them to be."

Then Alexandre, who had been busy explaining just
how he had mixed up *neko-irazu* and *nezumi-irazu*, got
on the phone, saying right off the bat, "No word from
Tsuneko."

Fuyuhiko apparently said, "It's strange."

"What's strange?"

"You two siblings—and of course Natsuyuki and me
too—have such weak attachments to our parents." He was
struggling to contain his emotions.

"What the hell has that got to do with me? Don't you
mix me up in all this!" Alexandre said.

There was still lots of sashimi and other food and sake

on the table, and no one had touched Alexandre's home-made seaweed sushi roll. There was really quite a lot for me to think over. I felt, in a way, that my wanting to be the discoverer of original works that had not yet come to light might have been a kind of makeshift on my part. But it also occurred to me that there was something odd about my tendency always to regret things and blame myself for them. I felt that there was no longer any reason for me to go to New York but also that I could still go just for the fun of it, unrelated to my earlier project. Trying to spare the left molar that had partly crumbled away earlier, I was chewing at the raw turbo in such a way that I bit the inside of my left cheek along with the turbo. When, afterward, I looked at the inside of my mouth with one of those little mirrors some people use when they brush their teeth, I found a blood blister about the size of a small grain of rice there.

The girls from next door had found an interesting topic, whispering and giggling among themselves, and from the veranda came the landlady's voice: "Excuse me! I thought our Nora might be paying you a visit. . . . "

"She's sleeping with our Tama," I answered.

"Nora is still so attached to Tama!" the landlady laughed. "I hate to wake her up, but I'll just take her back home with me." I picked Nora up and handed her over. "Why, Nora, your tummy looks fit to burst! Did you eat lots of goodies at Natsuyuki's house today? You are a shrewd one, aren't you?"

"Tama's always getting lots of treats at your house, so she's the shrewd one, I'd say," I said.

"My, how good that smells! You're cooking turbo in the shell, aren't you? This wonderful smell brought you here, didn't it, Nora?"

I knew, of course, that the landlady was not angling for some turbo by saying this, and I knew too that if invited to take some home with her, she'd say: "Oh, our teeth are so bad now—just the smell is enough for us!" So I placed two pieces of horse mackerel and some pickled wasabi on a plate and asked her to please have some.

"There's some *tade* growing next to the well in the back garden, so if you're going to grill your horse mackerel with salt, I'll make some *tade* vinaigrette and bring it over."

"Oh, *tade* vinaigrette . . ."

"'Some like *tade*, and some don't,' as the saying goes, so I'm not at all sure that young people like you will like it but . . ."

"No, I like it, and I haven't had any for a long, long time."

"Well, in that case, I'll make some and bring it right over." Then, with a kitten in one hand and a dish in the other, she sat down on the veranda. "My, my! The writer lady is resting! She must be very tired."

So, there was some *tade* growing by the old well in the back garden. I'd recalled only the other day how, long ago, I'd eaten horse mackerel grilled with salt with a *tade* vinaigrette dressing. It must have been right after Ma left home. (I don't have any clear memory of when it was. Was I in primary school by then? How old was I? Was I in school? It could have been during summer vacation.)

"When the hell did you run out on us? And how old was I at the time?" I'd ask, and Ma would give one of her evasive answers: "Now let me see . . . What year would that have been? Whenever it was, you were already a big boy, I'm sure of that. No point worrying about it now." Evasive and convenient.

Dad once took me here and there, looking for Ma, trying to figure out where she might be. It was a terribly hot summer, and in the various gardens we visited and in empty lots in alleyways or by the roadside, huge sunflowers, much taller than I was, were blooming ferociously, like some sort of bright yellow wild animal. From inside the dark walls around the various houses, gaudy pink oleander blossoms were in full bloom, and their confetti ball-like clusters swayed heavily in the hot wind as the large, narrow leaves of the deep orange canna plants became covered with dust.

As Dad and I rode trains and taxis and walked along the streets, hot, sand-like dust was blown against our faces, hands, and feet. From house to house we went, until—where was it?—perhaps the home of a friend from Ma's girls' school days—I found myself in a house with a large garden, where I fed bread to the carp in the pond until it was time to go home, taking along some *tade* that the lady of the house had picked in the garden. Yes, she had given us some watermelon that had been chilled in the well before we left. Dad bought some horse mackerel at a fish shop that day, and we grilled it on a portable stove in our garden and ate it dipped in *tade* vinaigrette.

There had been *tade* growing by the well, and the lady, wearing a quiet, almost mannish cotton *yukata*, pulled the watermelon up from the well, ignoring the bites of the large mosquitos there. Then she wrapped up some *tade*, put it into a plastic bag, and gave it to us, I remembered.

Tama woke up, yawned, and came slowly toward the veranda. As I stroked her, she brought her nose close to the dish the landlady was holding and sniffed at it. "Oh, Tama dear!" she cried, and then, as if suddenly remembering, said, "There's *tade* growing by the old well. When we built these apartments, we filled in the well along with the pond that was here. The well water wasn't of very good quality to begin with, so we just used it to chill watermelons in summertime." She sighed, and I felt a slight dizziness, suddenly realizing that *this was the place* and that, if that were so, my mother and the landlady must know one another.

Alexandre, still holding the receiver, said politely to the landlady, "Those ricebran pickles you gave us the other day were really delicious!" Then, speaking into the receiver again, he said, "Okay, I'll tell you what's what. Sis's in Alexandria . . . Yeah, that's right—Alexandria in Egypt, the ancient city founded by Alexander the Great. . . . No, I don't know her exact address. She's running a brothel there," he explained. "She's got quite a few boys. She's wild for them herself, and she's making out like a bandit from the tourists who come. . . . Yeah, she phoned to ask if I'd come out and give her a hand, but I turned her down—just didn't feel like it. It would be one thing to go for a visit, but I just don't feel like going and working at a brothel with underage boys, you know? Why don't you go to Egypt and look for her yourself? . . . Yeah. . . . Yeah. . . . So is that it, then? . . . Okay? You don't need to talk to Natsuyuki? . . . Oh, you *do*? . . . Okay, hang on a sec."

I took the receiver, and Fuyuhiko asked if what Alexandre had just said was true or not, sounding as if he found it very difficult to trust him.

"Gee, it's hard for me to say," I answered.

"I bet he was makin' it up as he went along, just havin' fun at my expense. Because what he said is ridiculous! It's, well, just plain ridiculous!" All this was delivered at high speed, and then he fell silent. Since I had nothing to say, I kept silent too. Then Fuyuhiko began sobbing. I imagined him clutching the receiver on the other end. What could I do?

"Alexandre's saying that he *was* lying, just to tease you a bit," I lied. But Fuyuhiko kept right on sobbing, and, feeling a little frightened, I said soothingly, "So I'm going to hang up now. You take care."

Having ended the call, I turned on Alexandre: "Now listen you, stop teasing that poor guy! He was crying so hard I didn't know what to do!" Alexandre was completely unaffected and started rehashing the business of how he came to confuse *neko-irazu* and *nezumi-irazu*. The girls from next door, however, having listened, open-mouthed, to what he'd said about the boys' brothel in Alexandria seemed to have lost all interest in the other matter, and just nodded perfunctorily as Alexandre talked on.

Our landlady, who had not yet gone to the rear garden to get the *tade* and had been sitting on the veranda listening all along, seemed not in the least suspicious of Alexandre's use of such rough Tokyo "low city" slang. "Why, of course! It must be awfully hard for a foreign gentleman to distinguish between *nezumi-irazu* and *neko-irazu*," she commented, laughing politely.

The girls, too, giving up, just laughed and said in a listless sort of way, "Yes, of course."

\* \* \*

Ignoring the surrounding turmoil—shall I say?—or at any rate unaffected by the many voices that were chattering on, the lady novelist continued sleeping, snoring as she did.

"She's got nerves of steel, she has!" Alexandre said.

"She's tired!" said Hanako from next door, sympathetically.

Momoko, the writer's niece who had spent a year living with her auntie, was inclined to take Alexandre's view: "She's always like this. Even if she isn't tired, once she's fallen asleep, it's hard to wake her up."

Then Alexandre had an idea: "I've got a pirated video that the porn director brought me as a present from Hong Kong. He said it's quite unusual. Let's watch it."

"Porn?"

"I'm not sure about that. The title's in Chinese, and

you can't tell what it's about from the picture here on the case."

"Yeah. *Jojinjūkarifukuniya*, it says" I read, using the Sino-Japanese pronunciation of the Chinese characters.

"Could 'karifukuniya' be 'California'?"

"Very clever! Well done, for a dish girl."

"What's that mean?"

"That's the word for young girls in Chinese, apparently. But what about this *jojinjū* business? Is it, like, 'Women follow after California'?"

"Sure. It's a story about Chinese immigration to California," I suggested. "Look, the picture on the case shows a young girl wearing a kind of turban on her head. She's the completely Americanized second-generation daughter of the owner of some dry cleaner or chop suey place who's made a success of himself and then sent his child to be educated at UCLA. She falls in love with this Jewish-American guy who looks a lot like Woody Allen, glasses and all, but there's a clash of cultures: He can't eat Chinese food because he's Jewish! So there's trouble with the family, treated in a comic way, but in the end everything works out fine. That's what I think it'll be!"

"Hmm, I wonder. Why aren't there any Chinese in the picture then?" Momoko said, looking doubtful.

"Yeah, but the title's *got* to mean Californianized women," I insisted, even though I didn't believe it myself.

The other three said they couldn't accept that. "This girl in the turban isn't a California type at all!"

"Hey, dummies. This isn't a contemporary story. It's from the '30s or '40s. Didn't you guys see *Chinatown*? Faye Dunaway was wearing a turban just like this!" I was getting more and more insistent. "Anyway, watch it and then you'll see. I don't think it'll be very entertaining, though." I inserted the cassette into the deck.

Woody Allen's name appeared on the screen right

away, and my reaction was: Just as I thought! Then Diane Keaton's name appeared and, separated from it by a tiny "in," came the title: *A Girl from California*. All three of us burst out laughing. There were no more titles; the movie proper started right away. It was set in New York, not California, and both Woody Allen and Diane Keaton were chattering away in extremely high-pitched, rapid Chinese. They smoked lots of cigarettes or pipes and were living together in an apartment awash with books. They seemed to be New York intellectuals.

Then this young girl, an acquaintance of the Keaton character's, arrives from California. I didn't recognize the actress, but she was a lively, clever-looking young woman. The girl starts to live in the same building as the couple, on one of the lower floors. She quickly becomes popular in her new circle of acquaintances. In time, Woody Allen, who makes a living as a professor or something, is attracted to her. Diane Keaton gets jealous, but she too finds a lover, apparently a writer, and younger than herself.

At this point Alexandre got bored and started to complain: "This is a big nothing. Let's turn it off." The lady novelist, who had apparently awakened from her nap and had been watching the video from a certain point on, said, "You know, this must be—of course I don't understand a word of the Chinese, but I think it must be Simone de Beauvoir's *She Came to Stay*. Just wait and see. Soon Sartre, as played by Woody Allen, will start wandering the corridors and then peek into the girl's bedroom."

And sure enough, there was such a scene. We all applauded. On the black-and-white screen, Diane Keaton, playing Beauvoir watching Sartre peeking into the girl's room from the top of the stairs, is shown in close-up with the actress making a valiant effort to assume a subtle, complex expression on her face. Well, it wasn't very interesting anymore, so we fast-forwarded and looked at the final credits. The film was based on Beauvoir's novel *She Came to Stay*. "See?" said the lady novelist, with a derisive snort. "That Woody Allen—what a dummy he is!"

Then we ate the salt-grilled horse mackerel with the *tade* dressing the landlady had brought over, and the homemade seaweed sushi rolls. The two girls from next door went home, promising to help clean up tomorrow, and the lady novelist left about five minutes after that. "What do you want to do?" I asked Alexandre.

"If everybody leaves at once, you'll be lonesome, so I'll spend the night here," he replied.

"Yeah, that'll be okay."

"Just 'okay'? How cold!"

The room was filled with the smells of grilled fish and turbo, and the sink was full of glasses and greasy dishes. The food waste container and wastebasket were filled to over-flowing with turbo and abalone shells. It was a depressing scene. Should I put all the shells into a Styrofoam box and plan to put them out on a "non-burnable garbage" day? As I pondered this and sipped a beer, Alexandre made some space amid the stuff on the floor, took some bedding from the closet, and started to spread it out.

"Whew! I'm bushed! You must be too. It's the first time you've worked for quite a while. You remember the woman who was driving the car this afternoon? I was planning on going to her place. She was in the video with me. Can you believe she was the female lead? A traditional pearl diver—that plain-looking, round-faced woman with her long, straight hair. I was a Spanish Jesuit who made it to shore alone after my ship sank in a storm, when Japan was closed to the outside world. . . . Give me a break!

"Anyway, the actress has just broken up with her lover, and she says, 'I live all by myself, so you can come stay with me if you like.' I decided to ignore her looks and move in. (Though judging from experience, these long-haired, moon-faced women are very jealous, and if they turn hysterical, they claw at you.) But when I asked if she liked cats, she said she hated them, that they were disgusting—all limp and hairy, that they dirty a room and are two-faced creatures. Well, she's just so extremely nasty about cats that I realized I couldn't take Tama to her place, and if I can't have Tama with me, why should I put up with this smelly cunt?

"I was reminded of the most important thing of all: There's no better environment in Tokyo for Tama than right here! And you're probably going off to New York soon. As soon as you get the three million yen from your dead fake-father's will, you'll be off, won't you? Well, Tama and I will look after the place for you while you're away! Doesn't that seem like a super-rational sort of plan? I'll take care of the rent for this place while you're gone, too." This was Alexandre's proposal as he lay stretched out in a pair of boxer shorts on top of the cotton blanket, busily scratching away at his golden-tanned skin, which had begun to peel.

"Great idea, don't you think? Here you are in this sooty old apartment, cooking liver for the cat, combing out the tangles in her fur with a flea comb, and trying to make a little money by taking photos of some cheap novelist. Doesn't it make you sick? Hey, Natsuyuki, doesn't it?"

"Oh yeah," I said to myself, remembering. That summer when Ma ran out on us, her father was dying from a long, long illness, and even though it was a hot summer, the rheumatism in his left hand and foot became intensely painful if we put the air-conditioner on, so the old man was sleeping in a hot room cooled only slightly by a slowly moving electric fan. He absolutely refused to go into a hospital, so a nurse would spend the night with him, giving him injections of Ringer's solution, providing an oxygen mask, etc.

Granny stated with stiff formality, "I no longer regard Tsutayo as in any way our daughter, and we're not going to look for her. If you happen to find her, Mr. Kobayashi, please don't bother to tell her anything about what's happening in this house." (I was told this story any number of times by Granny herself. And then I burst into tears, crying out, "Don't you speak badly of my mother, you nasty old hag!" *This* story I was told any number of times by my mother, as something she had heard from Granny.)

I don't remember any of that at all. But apparently an overweight doctor came straight into the guest parlor facing the garden and plumped down on the veranda. After gulping down the glass of ice water our maid had brought him, he looked up at the clear blue sky above the garden with its small pond, some stagnant greenish water collecting near the bottom, folded his arms over his chest and muttered, "Yup, a good rain'd help our patient improve, but . . ." Or so I've been told.

Why, I don't know, but later on my father did an imitation of the doctor many times: "'A good rain'd help him improve . . .' Well then, humans and plants are much the same!" Dad would say with a laugh. That's why I remembered it. "Well then, humans and plants are much the same" was fine, but Dad always added, "The roots have to go deep into the earth, from which they must absorb moisture and nutrients, or they can't survive." Ridiculous, you'd have to say.

I have no idea what happened to Dad after that. Ma gave incoherent explanations like: "You see, Kobayashi ran off with a girl from his office. (She always wore a navy-blue duster and kept her curly, reddish hair pulled back tight. Her face had a sad, brooding look to it. She looked a lot like—what was her name now?—oh yes, Kobayashi Toshiko, the actress. She seemed a little mean, somehow.) And that's why I left you with Granny and went and found a job." An odd account, but I don't care about that anymore.

Recalling the sentence "Humans and plants are much the same," I also remembered a photograph with an explanation attached: "The Anderson children in the greenhouse at our summer home in Newport." A single photo taken by Amanda with her father's camera when she was ten years old. I don't know what they're called, but there's an array of tropical-looking plants with big, thick, sword-shaped leaves, large prickly water lilies, bananas and pineapples and other plants of the same kind growing en masse together. And half-hidden among them, in trompe l'oeil style, can be seen Amanda's brothers and sisters and three cousins. The children's arms and legs, revealed by their bathing costumes, are interlaced like the vines of some plant, and some of the children are blurred, as if they had tired of keeping still during the long exposure time required. But that makes them look all the more like vines shaken by the wind in this very strange photograph. "The play of light and shadow. A time lost forever comes back to life in the darkroom," writes Swanson. That's how she writes, as if she herself had done the developing.

These thoughts of mine may be the result of baseless envy, and I feel I could easily come up with a pseudo-psychoanalytic explanation of such feelings of envy and desire: that my desire to develop and print the unreleased rolls of Amanda Anderson's film may actually be a fear of taking photographs of my own. That conclusion would probably make me feel most comfortable of all.

"Well, that's all okay too. But, you know, everybody's different. You don't have to be so serious about it, Natsuyuki." With that, Alexandre fell asleep, clutching the cotton blanket.

The next morning, saying he had some business or other, Alexandre left early, and the girls next door who'd said they'd help clean up that day all had hangovers and stayed in bed until after noon. They showed their faces around 3:00 p.m.

"You must have cleaned up already, huh?" they asked with girlish curiosity. "But, say, was that true—what Alexandre said on the phone yesterday—about his sister? Was it?"

"That was a pack of lies," I answered, and the girls looked a bit disappointed.

"Well, I wouldn't be surprised if it *was* true," they said to one another.

"Of course, one wouldn't be surprised—it seems quite possible, in fact," I continued.

Somehow that seemed to remind them of last night's video, and they both cried out, laughing, "We don't believe anything you say, Natsuyuki! You just say whatever comes to mind. It's a disgusting thing to do!" Then, "We're going to see a Joseph Cornell exhibition in Takeshiba. Will you come with us?"

"I've already seen it. Why don't you ask your auntie to go?"

"She said she saw it on the first day."

"Oh, yeah?"

Off they went, as Tama, back from an excursion, settled in on the veranda. She raised one hind leg way up as far as her ears, spread her front legs out, planted her feet on the floor, bent her neck around and began to lick the fur on her belly and the scar from her sterilization operation. After dealing attentively with that task, she brought the tip of her raised hind leg to her mouth, spread her toes wide, and, wrinkling her nose, removed the dirt that had collected between her toes and claws with her tongue and teeth. When she had finished cleaning all four paws like this, she bent her neck way around and licked at the fur on her back. That done, she moistened the tips of her front paws by licking them with her tongue and started to give her face a thorough washing. Then she plopped down on her side and, looking at me, gave two "Rrawrs," started to purr, and was soon fast asleep. Even though she had washed her face, a dark brown gum remained in the inner corner of each eye, which I removed with a fingertip. "If you leave gum here like this, you'll look like a lazy cat, Tama!" I found myself talking to the slumbering cat.

I was lying on the tatami half-asleep when the lady novelist entered by the garden gate, announcing she had just come back from the bookstore. "My, but Tama manages to sleep a lot! Oh, I'm so thirsty. D'you have any beer?" I brought out a can of beer. "A glass too, please." Having drunk her beer, she started to talk: "I'd forgotten all about it, but then yesterday, looking at Alexandre, I remembered. Did you know about Tsuneko?"

What she had to say was largely the same as what Alexandre had told Fuyuhiko on the phone the previous night, except that the news had come from a freelance editor friend whom the lady writer had met by chance in front of the monastery of San Marco or somewhere, and who had herself just come to Florence from Alexandria.

According to the freelance editor, it was well known among some people that Tsuneko was living in a certain area on the outskirts of Cairo, though the lady writer herself had not known it until she met her freelance editor friend in Florence. And there were of course some who knew also that Tsuneko had a young Arab lover, though those in the know were limited to two or three very close women friends of Tsuneko's. Her lover was a slim, handsome, brown-skinned lad with large eyes. Nobody knew what kind of work he had been doing in Italy. He had returned to Egypt, and Tsuneko had decided to live there too, apparently.

As she talked, the freelance editor played with the silver and turquoise ring she had bought in Egypt: "At the time, her women friends thought this torrid love story represented a courageous choice on the part of Tsuneko. The feeling was, 'Go for it, Tsuneko, and be happy!' Well, it was, after all, a new departure for a woman of forty, and with a guy ten to twenty years younger—her very own Arabian stallion!" A sigh escaped her.

"Of course, we had an idea that Tsuneko had built up her nest-egg by shady means," the freelance editor had admitted. "But women have the right to do such things for themselves when they need to."

"Sure they do," replied the lady writer. "What happened after that?"

"We girls had planned a trip to Cairo in April, to visit Tsuneko." Then, after pussyfooting around the subject for a while, she came out with: "Oh, I think I can tell *you*. Tsuneko said she could introduce us to cute Arab boys around fourteen to eighteen years of age.

"You could just give them a tiny sum of money and that would be that, she said. Well, when we actually got there, the 'tiny sum of money' turned out to be for their tips. 'If you really want a good time, of course you'll need some funds. We have all our boys checked for AIDS and other venereal diseases, and the boys themselves aren't doing it for the fun of it. Their livelihoods—and the livelihoods of their families—depend on this.' So she sort of threatened us, and then jacked up the prices to way over fair market-level," the freelance editor complained.

"How much were you overcharged?" asked the lady writer.

"About ten times the going rate!" was the furious reply. "I almost fell over laughing. Tsuneko *is* dependable, after all. She should have overcharged them even more!" The lady writer burst out laughing again. "If Alexandre got it into his head to go to Cairo, I bet she'd put him to work with the other boys. And it wouldn't bother him a bit!"

It wasn't particularly out of kindness, but I decided not to share all this with Fuyuhiko.

"What happened with the Amanda Anderson thing?" the lady novelist asked, and after I'd explained what I'd been told about the Paris publication the previous day, she said, "I see" and fell silent for a while. "But maybe it's all for the best. . . . Yes, I think it is," she said, and left for home.

So, in the end, I accomplished nothing with respect to Amanda Anderson's photography. A young Japanese critic wrote about her photographs as hot news in one of the magazines, and it seems a collection of her photographs may be published here. I, of course, did not have a monopoly on her photos, nor did I discover them. I just happened to find them by chance on the shelf of a secondhand bookstore. The fact that *Zoom* put together a special issue and that her unpublished works have now been collected and published is certainly no skin off my nose.

I was feeling drowsy and must have dropped off without knowing it when I was awakened by the sound of torrential rain. I closed the glass door to the veranda, where the rain was blowing in, and was looking into the darkness outside and having a smoke when a man drenched to the skin raced up and began pounding with both hands on the rain-pelted glass door, shouting something I couldn't make out. I had a vague premonition that turned out to be on target: It was, of course, a soaking-wet Fuyuhiko. I led him to the bathroom. He splashed water on the veranda and six-mat room and four-and-a-half-mat room and kitchen as we passed through the apartment. I gave him a bath-towel and a tee-shirt and cotton pants to change into, and then wondered what was up, as I mopped up the water from the now-wet veranda and tatami.

Fuyuhiko emerged from the bathroom, drying his hair with the towel after having changed into the dry clothes. He sat down in the same spot that he had silently established as his own while staying with me, where he could lean back comfortably against my bookcase. What could I do but ask him if he wouldn't like something nice and warm to drink? Shivering, Fuyuhiko asked for some really hot roasted green tea.

"You *did* take a hot shower, I hope," I said with mother-like concern. I was determined not to touch on the subject of Tsuneko until he brought it up. As I put the teakettle on, Tama could be heard outside yowling in a high-pitched voice, "Rrawr, rrawr, rrawr." I hurriedly opened the door, and the mud-covered cat bounded into the room, looking like a half-drowned rat. She shook herself all over, sending the none-too-clean moisture that had collected in her fur flying throughout the room. I wrapped her in a towel and dried her off as best I could. She responded with very pleased, affectionate purring.

I gave Tama her milk and Fuyuhiko his roasted green tea. It seemed that when he was in a closed room where the humidity had risen rapidly, he sweated profusely, even with the air conditioner on. There was a mixture of strong odors in the room: the smell of burnt fat from the grilled fish, a feral smell from Tama's wet fur, the fragrance of the eau de cologne that Fuyuhiko had apparently splashed on his neck (an unwanted note if there ever was one), and the reek of the bourbon he must have been drinking on the Super Express from Kyoto. Plus, there arose from Fuyuhiko's wet and wrinkled blue suit, which was hanging on the veranda, the smell of wet cloth, mingling odors of sweat and cologne and highly unpleasant dirtiness. The telephone rang. It was Alexandre, shouting in a loud voice so as to be heard over the noise of the rain and cars in the background. "It's me! I'm at Mejiro Station now, but with this damn rain—why don't you just come to the station, and we'll have dinner out?"

"Okay, I'll be right there," I answered.

I was on my way out, but the thought of seeing Alexandre's face made me mad, and yet I didn't feel like going back to my apartment either. So I decided, for want of anything better to do, to go to the lady writer's condominium. She wasn't home, though, and out into the rain I went again. Entering a coffee shop on Mejiro Avenue, I considered where to go.

After all, the pictures I'd taken yesterday had to be developed before noon tomorrow, and I had to make ten 5 x 7 prints too. . . .

# *On* Oh, Tama!—
## *In Lieu of an Afterword*

Of all the different types of markings seen in cats, I like
dappled black and white best because that was the kind
of coat that Piyo, the tom who had lived with us since I
was an infant, had. Tama is like Piyo in her markings, the
length of her tail, and her beautiful green eyes. But Piyo
was far more elegant, intelligent, sensitive, and beautiful a
cat. There is no limit to the examples I could give to prove
Piyo's intelligence, but that really has nothing to do with
this novel, of course.

Just as the title of this series of stories is borrowed
from Uchida Hyakken's *Oh, Nora!*,[1] as the Japanese reader
will have realized, so too the various chapter headings are
taken from the titles of other novels and poetry collec-
tions. "The Gift" comes from *Tamamono*, the Japanese
translation of the title of the novel by Nabokov;[2] "Wandering Soul" from *Hyōhaku no tamashii*, the Japanese
translation of the title of the novel *A Charmed Life* by
Mary McCarthy[3] (not at all a bad novel, by the way,
though *The Group* is of considerably greater interest);
"Evanescence" from *Tamayura* by Kawabata Yasunari[4]
(though there is also a modern poem with this title);
"Balls of Confetti" from *Kusudama*, an anthology of the
poetry of Yoshioka Minoru;[5] and—to be a little too
explanatory—the sound "tama" occurs in the Japanese
titles of all these works.

"Amanda Anderson's Photographs" is the sole excep-
tion to this rule. Had I given her the Slavic name "Tamara"
or the Spanish "Tamayo," it might have seemed too studied, but at least "tama" would have appeared in every title.

But Amanda Anderson is Amanda Anderson: That is an unalterable fact.[6]

Had it not been for copyright problems, I would have liked to have used one of Amanda Anderson's photos for the novel's cover. Fortunately, I was able to use a photo of Anna Karina taken by Yamada Kōichi;[7] and it happened to be *very like* the one printed by the protagonist of my novel. It appears on the front cover of this volume:[8] truly a fortunate convergence of coincidences.

As for the theme of the novel, briefly put, it would seem meaningless to search for the identity of the father of a child who has come into this world, whether in the case of cats or of humans. It is the same with the question of one's own real identity as well.

The father of the photographer Amanda Anderson was a well-known amateur photographer. According to her biography, he committed suicide when she was eighteen. Her biographer seems to imply that he suffered from mental illness.

More recent research into her life has given rise to other dramatic speculations about her, but of course nothing is known for certain. I wonder, for example, whether it is appropriate to conclude, through psychoanalytic interpretation of her photos, that there was incest involved. She appears to have been on quite good terms with her father—she learned the art of photography from him. But even so, it wouldn't change the theme of this novel.

We see lonely characters who were raised in broken homes or highly irregular families secretly tending to each other's forlorn souls. We see characters who live precariously, like floating weeds, who don't belong to traditional fictional worlds—like one in which someone searches for his father and then kills him. Initially, their lives seem frivolous and empty, yet as the author I would like to note that the more frivolous they are, the bitterer those lives are too.

Finally, I wish to both apologize and express my gratitude to those authors (and translators) whose titles I have borrowed for use in this novel.

I hope this novel will, like Tama's kittens, be well treated and cared for by those into whose hands it is entrusted.

*Kanai Mieko*
*September 19, 1987*

## *Afterword to the Paperback Edition (1999)*

In my afterword to the original 1987 edition of *Oh, Tama!* I wrote: "Of all the different types of markings seen in cats, I like dappled black and white best" because that was the kind of coat that Piyo, my cat from childhood days, had had. That was a conclusion I arrived at after considerable thought at the time, but one's ways of thinking change, after all.

One day, more than a year after the publication of *Oh, Tama!*, a very large tabby kitten with black stripes suddenly appeared at our apartment. We named him Toraa,[9] and since starting to care for him—or starting to *have* to care for him—my tastes have changed: I would now insist that black-striped tabbies are the handsomest of cats.

In my "Mejiro tetralogy",[10] the relationships among the characters are ruled by "coincidence," that chance factor deemed impermissible in twentieth-century fiction. It governs their coming together and their parting. This has been characterized by critics as careless or slapdash (which they mean as the highest praise). When one's novel is praised by critics, regardless of the accuracy or inaccuracy of the criticism, one must accept it with gratitude, criticism being a constant concomitant to the work of the active writer.

And yet, I must point out that the characters in *Oh, Tama!* are based on people who actually exist—a thing very rare in my fiction. The episodes that seem so slapdash, so glaringly all-too-convenient for the author's purposes, could hardly have been written, even by so brazen an author as myself, were there no guarantee that they had actually occurred.

Though the world of *Oh, Tama!* is made up of a series of events seen, heard, or experienced by the author and not taken from books, language, or cinema, still, there is no such thing as a novel written haphazardly, without calculation or planning.

Should I, then, make clear which sections are the result of cautious and detailed planning and calculation and which are accounts of actual occurrences that caused me, as the author, to say in amazement, "Surely *this* could not really have happened?"

No, of course there is no need for that.

For me, the most interesting aspect of writing this novel lay in the question of how to handle the "raw materials," which are powerful to the point of absurdity—such as a series of incidents, those actual yet undeniably strange occurrences the results of which I knew before writing the novel, and the relationships among Alexandre, Tsuneko, Natsuyuki, and Fuyuhiko and their respective mothers, whose memories are so notably poor.

Therefore I feel I can claim that I have "matured as a novelist" through writing this work.

Finally, in this afterword to the paperback edition of *Oh, Tama!*, a work full, for me, of many memories and recollections, I would like once again to offer my thanks

to those who permitted me to use them as models, kindly
saying, "Yes, go right ahead!"

*KM*

NOTES

1   Uchida Hyakken (1889–1971) was a writer and professor of
German, noted for his humorous writings as well as his love for
cats. *Nora ya* (Oh, Nora!, 1957) depicts the pathetic state of the
author, totally distraught when his beloved cat, Nora, so named
because he was a stray cat (*nora neko*), disappears. In *Kuru ya,
omae mo ka* (Oh, Kurtz, You Too!, 1963), the old master finds
happiness in another cat, Kurtz, who looks like Nora, but this
cat, too, causes much grief when he dies. Hyakken (usually
referred to by this pen name), was a student of the renowned
writer Natsume Sōseki and also wrote a humorous sequel to his
teacher's celebrated novel titled *Gansaku wagahai wa neko de
aru* (I Am a Cat: A Sham).

2   *The Gift* by Vladimir Nabokov was written in Russian in the
mid-1930s while Nabokov was living in Berlin.

3   *A Charmed Life*, published 1955.

4   The Nobel laureate Kawabata Yasunari (1899–1972) wrote
a short story entitled "Tamayura" in 1951. Later he wrote
another and longer novel of the same title, which was serialized
between 1965 and 1966. The title consists of two components,
*tama* (ancient jewels or beads) and *yura* (sway). Although the
combination is believed to signify momentary beauty, the exact
meaning of the compound word cannot be determined and is
hence well suited to Kawabata's aestheticism, which is full of
ambiguity.

5   Yoshioka Minoru (1919–1990) was an acclaimed poet and book
designer. *Kusudama* is the title of his 1983 poetry anthology.

6   Many devoted Kanai readers, especially those who are interested in photography, have searched for this mysterious woman
photographer and the collection of her photographs mentioned
in this novel. In an interview conducted in 2006, Kanai revealed
to the interviewer, Taguchi Kenji, who had tried to find a copy
of the Amanda Anderson book in overseas bookshops, that the

photographer existed only in a very vivid dream Kanai once had. See Kanai Mieko, *Shōsetsuron*, Tokyo: Asahi Shinbun Shuppan, Asahi Bunko, 2008, p. 238. See also Atsuko Sakaki's essay "Photography as Corporeal Reproduction: Swapping Pregnancy for Photography in Kanai Mieko's *Tama ya*" in *Poetica*, 78 (2012), pp. 49–68.

7  Yamada Kōichi (b. 1938) is a film critic who lived in Paris in the mid-1960s and had close associations with the leading figures of the French *nouvelle vague*, including Jean-Luc Godard, François Truffaut, and Anna Karina. As Sakaki shows, the hardcover edition of *Tama ya* used a photograph of Anna Karina taken by Yamada and originally used for a cover of his book. See Sakaki 2012, Figures 1 and 2, and the interesting further account involving Anna Karina's photographs.

8  This refers to the 1987 original hard cover edition of *Tama ya*. Descriptions such as "very like" and "a fortunate convergence of coincidences" present further examples of Kanai writing as a tongue-in-cheek, intentional "trickster."

9  Kanai Mieko and her artist sister Kumiko have produced numerous works inspired by, and as a tribute to, this cat. The name is sometimes spelled Tora, a common name for tiger-striped cats. The version with a longer vowel is a reference to the name of the tiger cub, Tigger, in the Japanese translation of A. A. Milne's *Winnie the Pooh*.

10  The Mejiro tetralogy refers to *Bunshō kyōshitsu* (Creative Writing Class, 1985), *Tama ya* (Oh, Tama!, 1987), *Indian Summer* (1988, English translation 2012), and *Dōkeshi no koi* (A Clown's Love, 1990). The tetralogy has expanded into the Mejiro series with additional books: *Kanojo(tachi) ni tsuite watashi ga shitte iru 2, 3 no kotogara* (Two or Three Things I Know about Her [and Others], 2000), and *Kaiteki seikatsu kenkyū* (A Study of the Comfortable Life, 2006). While *Okatte taiheiki* (Kitchen Chronicles, 2014) is not set in Mejiro, several characters from the Mejiro series appear.

# *Contributors*

ABOUT THE AUTHOR

**Kanai Mieko** (b.1947) has steadily produced poetry, fiction, and criticism of a very high order since making her literary debut in her teens. In 1967 she was runner-up for the Dazai Osamu Prize for *Ai no seikatsu* (A Life of Love), and the following year she received the Gendai-shi Techō Prize for poetry. In 1979 she was awarded the Izumi Kyōka Prize for *Puraton-teki ren'ai* (Platonic Love), and in 1988 she received the Women's Literature Award for *Tama ya* (*Oh, Tama!*). Her most recent novel, *Kasu-toro no shiri* (The Ass of Castro, 2017), whose title plays on Stendhal's *L'Abbesse de Castro*, was awarded the 2018 Minister of Education's Award. While maintaining a certain distance from literary circles and journalism, she has created her own world of fiction that mixes the sensual with humor, beauty, and horror, nostalgia with realism, the highbrow with the popular. Along with her fiction, her film and literary criticism, demonstrating scathing insight and wide-ranging erudition, also has a devoted following.

ABOUT THE TRANSLATORS

**Tomoko Aoyama** received a Ph.D. from the University of Queensland, Australia, where she is Associate Professor of Japanese. She is the author of *Reading Food in Modern Japanese Literature* and numerous book chapters, journal articles, and conference papers. She has also co-edited *Girl Reading Girl in Japan* and *Configurations of Family in Contemporary Japan* and translated Kanai Mieko's novel

*Indian Summer* (with Barbara Hartley) and a number of critical essays and short stories.

**Paul McCarthy** received a Ph.D. in East Asian Languages and Civilizations from Harvard University with a dissertation on Tanizaki Jun'ichirō. He has taught Japanese and English language and literature and comparative literature at universities in the US and Japan, and was Visiting Professor at the International Center for Japanese Studies in Kyoto. He is Professor Emeritus of Comparative Culture, Surugadai University, and lives in Tokyo. He has written studies of Tanizaki Jun'ichirō, Mishima Yukio, and Nakajima Atsushi and has translated numerous works, including *Childhood Years*, *A Memoir* and *A Cat, a Man, and Two Women and Other Stories* by Tanizaki Jun'ichirō and *101 Modern Japanese Poems* (edited by Ōoka Makoto).